Secret of Goblin Glen

WESTMINSTER PRESS BOOKS BY
Phyllis A. Whitney

The Mystery of the Gulls
Mystery of the Black Diamonds
Mystery on the Isle of Skye
Mystery of the Green Cat
Secret of the Samurai Sword
Mystery of the Haunted Pool
Secret of the Tiger's Eye
Mystery of the Golden Horn
Mystery of the Hidden Hand
Secret of the Emerald Star
Mystery of the Angry Idol
Secret of the Spotted Shell
Mystery of the Strange Traveler
Secret of Goblin Glen

SECRET
of *GOBLIN GLEN*

BY

Phyllis A. Whitney

ILLUSTRATED BY AL FIORENTINO

The Westminster Press
PHILADELPHIA

LIBRARY OF CONGRESS CATALOG CARD NO. 68–10236

BOOK DESIGN BY
DOROTHY ALDEN SMITH

Published by The Westminster Press
Philadelphia, Pennsylvania ®

PRINTED IN THE UNITED STATES OF AMERICA

Contents

1 *My Infamous Ancestor*

UNTIL this afternoon, when I arrived in Camberhills for the first time, I've always thought it interesting to have a black sheep great-uncle on the family tree. What happened nearly forty years ago seemed like a story to me — far away and romantic. A little as if I were distantly related to Billy the Kid.

Of course I never knew my Great-uncle Will Horst because he died long before I was born. When he was young he and another man, Burt Boyd, held up the Putney Bank in Camberhills and stole an awful lot of money. Both men were caught and went to prison, and Mother says her family felt so disgraced they never got over it.

There is still a mystery about what happened to the money Will Horst and Burt Boyd took from the bank. Though they were caught in a few days, the money was never found. I suppose the sensible part of my mind told me that if no one had found the money in the forty years since the robbery, then I certainly wasn't going to. But just the same, I arrived in Camberhills with a dreamy notion at the back of my mind about being a real-life heroine and finding what no one else had ever been able to unearth.

My coming to Camberhills at all was an event in our family. After the disgrace of what his brother did, my grandfather had moved away and never gone back. So Mother was born in New York, instead of in New Hampshire, and she has never seen the family town. Only my great-grandfather stayed on to live down what his son had done. Great-uncle Will served his time in prison and came out to live a quiet life in another part of the country. If he knew where the money was, he never told, and the mystery of the lost wealth was never solved. Burt Boyd, who was the leader and the worst one of the two, had probably been mixed up in other robberies in the area. Eventually he died in jail in a fight with another prisoner—and he never told about the money either.

Before I left home on this unexpected summer visit, I asked my mother if Camberhills people would pay any attention if I came right out and told them I was descended from Will Horst. She said not to bring it up because it wasn't something to brag about and I'd just look silly. All the Camberhills Horsts were gone, and she hoped the whole story was forgotten by now.

While we were talking there at home Dad looked at me in the way he has—half affectionate, half despairing, and said, "Think, Trina. For once in your life think before you leap."

But dreaming of wonderful things I might do is a sort of thinking, isn't it? And of course nothing either of them said stopped me from wishing that I might be the one to find the lost money and return it, making up for what my ancestor had done.

Then, quite suddenly this afternoon, the whole thing began to seem close and real and quite awful—not something to make up pleasant daydreams about.

Mr. Myrick met my plane from New York when it came down in the little New Hampshire airport, but the rest of his family wasn't with him. He said in a wry sort of way that they were very busy on an important matter, and he hoped I wouldn't mind.

Hugh Myrick is a well-known writer of spy stories and his books are on all the paperback stands. He also writes an occasional hard-cover novel for my father, who is an editor at a big publishing house in New York. Mother and Mrs. Myrick are old college friends, and I had met both Mr. and Mrs. Myrick when they visited Manhattan. But since they were living in Philadelphia, I had never met their son and daughter, who are about my own age. That is, the girl is thirteen, like me, and the boy twelve.

I'm Trina Corey, by the way. Katrina is my real name — though I don't like it, so we've shortened it to Trina. I was named after my Great-grandmother Katrina Horst — the mother of that bank robber I was telling you about. I get my red hair from her too. It skipped my mother, who has pretty, dark, curly hair — while mine is straight and long and very red. I wear it down my back, or over my shoulders, with long bangs in front, and it wouldn't be much trouble that way, except for how it flies around and tangles.

The one thing I've inherited from my mother is my size. People sometimes take me for ten or eleven, which I don't like. Mother enjoys being little, but I don't. Sometimes Dad not only says, *"Think,"* to me; he also says, "Think *big."* I'm not sure that's good advice, because when I start "thinking big" I get into all sorts of trouble trying to make up for my size.

But to continue about my so-called looks. I have what storybooks call "a round, smiling face," and Mother says I have a warm heart and a fast temper. Right now I'm not so sure about the warm heart. Not since I've met Tex and Florida Myrick. I've begun to feel as though there might be a lot of mean revengefulness in me, and I'm trying to *think,* and not let my temper fly.

The reason I've come to Camberhills this July is a round-about one. Mother and Mrs. Myrick have kept in touch over the years, even though the Myricks have been living in all sorts of distant places. They came to Philadelphia only a year ago, and they quickly decided that a big city is too expensive and too crowded. Mr. Myrick finds that he writes best in a quiet place, and Dad has been encouraging him to think about a "serious novel" for the publishing list next year. So they looked around in New Hampshire and found a house in Camberhills, moving up there about four months ago.

Then Mother and Mrs. Myrick got this notion that it would be a fine thing for me to spend the summer vacation with the

Myricks—in the town of my forefathers—though that's my word, not theirs. Mother said that, after all, my Great-grandfather Fred Horst had been a respected citizen in the town, no matter what one of his sons did, and even though he died there long ago, Mother thought he would like it if his great-granddaughter returned for a visit. I thought it would be fun too. I never have much trouble making friends and I like to see new places and meet new people. Mother says I've never met a stranger—meaning that I act as though I know everybody. And since I'm an only child we both thought it a wonderful idea to have me spend the summer with another girl and boy.

Now I'm not so sure. I've met several strangers here who don't want me around. Wait till I tell you about Tex and Florida Myrick and what they did to me even before I'd had time to meet them.

First, though, the arriving part. In the Myricks' battered old station wagon we drove through rolling, hilly New Hampshire country. The real mountains start farther north, but there are plenty of hills around here. The town used to be a railroad stop long ago, but railroad travel ended, and the new highway bypassed the town, so Camberhills got lost. We had to take a side road off the highway for a few miles before we came into the town right on Main Street.

I guess I talked quite a lot on the way in, since Mr. Myrick was a good listener. On the plane I'd been thinking about Great-uncle Will Horst and the famous bank robbery, so while we were in the car I talked to him about that affair. I still thought the story was pretty romantic and I didn't dream then how fast I was going to change my mind about wanting people to know I was related to Will Horst. Mainly I was curious about the missing money and I wanted to find out more about what really happened. Mother says her father always hated to talk about it, so she never knew all the details.

Mr. Myrick listened to me without saying much. He isn't a handsome, distinguished-looking man like Dad, but he's nice-appearing in a quiet way, with brown eyes that really see you, as if he is thinking about you as a person. Maybe thinking about putting you into a story! He has a thin, rather gentle face, and he's not a very big man. You'd never expect to find him writing all that dangerous spy stuff. Before spies came in, he used to do Westerns and, being a writer, he and his family could live anywhere they liked. That's how Tex and Florida got their names—by being born in those two states. Mother often wonders what they'll do for a name if Marcia Myrick should have another child while she's living in New Hampshire.

When we reached Main Street we had to move slowly because there was some sort of building going on down the main block. Workmen were putting up a framework of arches over the street, and some of the townspeople were out in front of the small stores, watching and talking about what was going on.

I didn't have time to ask a question before Mr. Myrick said, "Folk Festival coming," and shook his head, looking gloomy. Then he added, "In this state selectmen manage the town government and as it happens we have a very—uh—progressive senior selectman here." I could see that he wasn't happy about that either. But before I could ask any questions he stopped the car at a parking meter, got out, and put in a nickel. He said he'd be right back, and disappeared through a door into a bank.

He hadn't said to stay in the car and I was eager to look around, so I hopped out and walked to the corner, looking back once in a while so I wouldn't miss Mr. Myrick when he came out. I liked the friendly look of the little street. Everyone seemed to know everyone else, and several people smiled at me—which doesn't often happen with people you don't know in New York City.

It wasn't a very long street because the high green slope of a hill cut right across it at the end, and the road continued uphill to the left, with another town street running around the base of the hill to the right. I could see the roofs of a few houses high up among the trees on the hill—and one big house in particular standing out very wide and creamy-white up there among all the green treetops.

At the end of the main block, with just one more block to go, I saw that a town square took up the space on my right. Set back in the center of it, with walks all around, was a fine old white clapboard building that seemed to be a meetinghouse. There was something going on inside right now because I could hear a voice coming through the open windows that sounded like someone speaking over a microphone. There were cars parked all around the square besides.

I turned back and saw that Mr. Myrick still hadn't come out of the bank, so I could take my time. Walking slowly, I looked into a shoe store window, a drugstore window, and the windows of a grocery store. Then I saw a sign on the front of the next building that said CAMBERHILLS PUBLIC LIBRARY. It looked just like the other stores, but there were books in the windows instead of shoes or groceries, and I stopped right there. I love libraries, and as soon as I could I would come down here and get a card in this one. Through the windows I could see a pretty young woman sitting at a desk working at a catalog file. Not a soul was in there getting books, and it was all I could do to keep from going inside then and there.

But out of the corner of my eye I saw Mr. Myrick come out of the bank and walk to the car. He looked surprised not to find me waiting for him in the front seat of the station wagon, so I scooted toward him. Or anyway, I tried to scoot. I ducked a man who came suddenly through a shop door, and then managed to trip over a board one of the workmen was sawing. That plopped me down on the sidewalk on my hands and knees, and from there I found myself looking straight at a wide green banner with lettering across it that another man was getting ready to carry up a ladder and string across the street. The words lettered across the green background were so astonishing that I stayed there on my hands and knees staring at them.

The banner said in foot-high letters: WELCOME BUDDY BROTHERS!

After all, I had often seen the two famous Buddy Brothers on television playing their guitars and singing, and I thought they were wonderful. They were American, but even better

than the Beatles, as far as I was concerned. When Mr. Myrick came up and helped me to my feet and asked if I was hurt, I could only point at the banner and jabber at him excitedly.

"Oh, no!" he said. "Not another one!" and looked as sad and gloomy as he had when he'd mentioned the senior selectman. "Let's get along home," he went on. "I can see this is going to be a hard summer."

"You mean because of the Buddy Brothers?" I asked, getting into the front seat beside him.

"Who else?" he asked, and ground his teeth at the same time that he ground the gears in starting. He seemed seriously upset, and I looked up at him, worried. I didn't want to have Mr. Myrick disturbed about something I had said. I liked him and I wanted him to like me. Maybe the very fact that he was more my size in the general scale of things made me have a special feeling toward him. I remembered that Marcia Myrick —Mrs. Myrick—was larger than her husband. Or anyway, wider.

We drove toward the end of the street, and when we passed the meetinghouse set in the middle of the little square, he waved a hand.

"My family is in there, and probably they're talking about these—these Buddy Brothers now. *Buddy Brothers!* Haven't these boys ever heard of redundancy?"

This was a word I knew, because of my father. Editors always love to pounce on redundant phrases in manuscripts— like "the big, large girl"—which is saying the same thing twice, unnecessarily.

"But it's a catchy name," I said. After all, I couldn't let my favorites down. Besides, it seemed very exciting that they were coming to town for the Folk Festival, and that I might get to see them in person.

"Catchy! That's what Florida says," Mr. Myrick admitted. "And that's why we seem to have offered our house to these two long-haired—uh, snails—or whatever they call themselves. There's no hotel here, and the nearest motel is miles away. Since Marcia wants to get into town activities and be a part of things, we've invited them to stay with us. Only there'll be no practicing on the premises, I can tell you."

I bubbled with laughter inside. I knew now that he was teasing me a little, just the way Dad did. If Florida liked the Buddy Brothers, then he would probably put up with them. Of course I hadn't seen Florida in action then. That made a difference in the sympathetic way I felt at the moment.

By now the car was at the end of the street and just before we turned, Mr. Myrick gestured toward the hill that rose above us.

"Did you notice the wide white house with the gables and towers up there? That's the place we've rented—with an option to buy. Of course we can't use the whole thing, but it's big enough so I can get clean away from the rest of the family to write. And that's especially important when the kids are home for the summer. By fall perhaps we'll know how both Camberhills and the house suit us. And how we suit them."

I loved the idea of staying in that big house high up the hill. There would be a wonderful view there, and all that room would be very different from a Manhattan apartment.

We took the left-hand turn, where the road ran uphill, and Mr. Myrick explained. "The other way gets us to the house more quickly, but I'm going around. There's something up here I'd like to show you."

The town seemed to peter out quickly, and in a few minutes we were on a blacktop country road. There were woods on both sides, with lots of pine trees and white birches, and I practically hung out of the car window enjoying everything, including the wonderful way the air smelled. More and more I was beginning to think this was going to be a terrific summer. Woods and outdoors! A library I could practically have to myself—*and* the Buddy Brothers! Who could ask for more?

Mr. Myrick spoiled my lovely mood. He slowed the car and pulled it off the road. "Let's get out," he said. "There's a lookout rock up here."

I didn't know what was coming and I got out right away. Sure enough, there was a gap in the trees, and the ground suddenly consisted of a big platform of rock, with dirt and gravel and pine needles ground into it. At the far edge a metal fence had been built to keep people from falling off the cliff. The view wasn't into the far distance as I expected, however. It was down into a deep cleft between steep rock cliffs that opened up in a stony valley at the bottom. There grassy earth spotted with great clusters of rock made the bed of the valley, and a stony brook, where a little stream of water still trickled, came out of nowhere, and went nowhere, disappearing underground.

The place was interesting, but I couldn't think why Mr. Myrick had brought me here before we went home. His first words, when we reached the metal fence, surprised me.

"What did you think of the bank?" he asked.

I blinked at him. "The bank?" For a minute I didn't know what he was talking about.

"Where we stopped back in town. The Putney Bank. Didn't you notice the name on the glass out in front?"

I hadn't noticed. There was no reason why I should look at the name of a bank. But Putney rang a bell, and I gaped at him.

"You mean—?"

"Yes," he said. "That's the bank you were telling me about all the way in from the airport. The one Will Horst and Burt Boyd held up. And right down there at the foot of this cliff is Goblin Glen."

Now he had lost me completely. I'd never heard of Goblin Glen. Of course I was interested in seeing the exact bank, but why this deep valley surrounded by cliffs should mean anything to me, I didn't know.

"Some families from Scotland settled this area originally, so you'll find the word 'glen' used hereabouts," Mr. Myrick said. "Someday perhaps I'll fictionalize the story of this place, robbery and all—if I can work out a satisfactory ending. The trouble with real-life stories is that they don't put themselves together neatly at the end. Down there is where Will and Burt hid out for two or three days with the money they took from the bank. The sheriff caught them when they tried to come out, but they didn't have a penny of it with them by that time.

Nor did they ever tell anybody what they did with it. That is —
not exactly."

I felt prickly with excitement. "And nobody ever found it!"
I cried, too thrilled just then to ask what he meant by "not
exactly."

"If anyone did, he never told," Mr. Myrick said, and I knew
he was watching me with that observing look, as though he was
testing me in some way. But all I could think about was my
Great-uncle Will and his partner hiding out down in this very
glen. Secretly digging, perhaps, or finding a ready-made rock
hiding place for the money. If no one had ever found it, then
it had to be there still.

"How do — " I stopped because the next word was going to
be "I" and it was better to change my wording. "How does a
person get down there?"

Mr. Myrick sighed as deeply as he had over the Buddy
Brothers. "That isn't exactly why I brought you here," he
said. "Trina Corey, I want you to think about something."

I looked at him, startled, and saw how solemn his brown
eyes were, and how his lips were pressed together without
any hint of a smile. He wasn't teasing now.

"I want you to forget about romantic treasure-hunting, and
about an ancestor who has taken on a bit of exciting glamour
over the years. A great many people were seriously injured by
that bank robbery, you know. Savings in banks weren't protected by the government in those days and some people lost
all they had. One man was completely ruined. I mean Andrew
Putney, who owned the bank. He never fully recovered from
what was done to him. Some of these people still live in Camberhills, including Mr. Putney, who is now a very old man.
These are real human beings, Trina. People who were hurt by
foolish boys turned criminal. Burt Boyd came from out of
town, but Will Horst belonged here. It was his own people
he injured. Innocent people. As a result, the name 'Horst'
isn't highly regarded in this town."

My throat had begun to choke up as I listened to him. He
sounded so serious and disapproving that I began to feel as
guilty as though I were responsible for that old bank robbery.

I couldn't understand why he was trying to make me feel un-
happy and ashamed, and I had to blink hard against the tears
that wanted to come into my eyes.

I think he saw this because he suddenly patted my shoulder
and stopped looking so grim. "There," he said, "don't worry
about what isn't your fault. I've done my duty. Your mother
wanted to make sure we got through to you about this being
a thing that really happened. It isn't a romantic story that you
can chat about cheerfully all around town. Though I don't
think your mother suspects how much feeling against Will
Horst there remains in this town. We didn't ourselves until
we began to inquire around a bit just before you came. Of
course we've told Tex and Florida the story, so they understand. And we can all forget about it. Every family has its
weaklings if you look hard enough. Trina, do you see what's
down there in the center of the glen? Geologically speaking,
it's an interesting place. Can you make out the goblins?"

I cheered up a little and leaned against the fence to stare in
the direction in which he was pointing. Right away I began to
see what he meant. All those strange rock shapes down there
really did look like goblins. For the first time I realized what
a scary place it was, quite aside from being a hiding place for
the lost money.

And at the same moment I knew with a queer sort of cer-
tainty that I was going down there. Goblins, or no, I had to
go down into this glen and see it close up for myself. Not
today—but soon.

2 *The Face in the Closet*

WHATEVER primitive waters, or glaciers, or crushing force had swept over this land millions of years ago, it had left some very odd rock formations down there between the cliffs. Perhaps a river had rushed through this narrow slot at one time. Anyway, ragged clusters of rock had been left behind when everything else was swept away. Mostly they all leaned in one direction — as if great pressure had pushed them into that position.

From where I stood I could see that they looked like scores of little men pressing forward desperately, hurrying as if to get somewhere — yet all the while standing perfectly still.

Somewhere not far off I heard the mechanical roar of a bulldozer, but when I looked around I couldn't find the source of the noise and I returned my attention to the deep cleft at my feet.

Except for weeds and scraggly grass that edged the trickle of remaining water, everything down there was a dark brown, earthy color. The brown, hurrying little figures seemed to wear caps or peaked hats and some of them possessed arms and legs and bodies carved out of rock. There were even what seemed to be strange little faces, though I couldn't make them out clearly from this distance. It was queer how groups of little goblin men clustered together here and there all over the glen, as if they sought protection as they hurried off together.

"I can see why it's called Goblin Glen," I said, shivering in bright sunlight.

The afternoon was getting late and while there was plenty
of light up here, down in the cleft the shadows grew long,
following the little figures in their endless running that didn't
go anywhere. "Can we get down there?" I asked.

"There used to be an easy way into the glen," Mr. Myrick
said. "Come over here and look."

He walked to the far edge of the platform rock, and as I
followed him the bulldozer roar sounded louder than before.

"About a hundred years ago there used to be a natural rock
camber across this chasm," Mr. Myrick said. "Some local
architect called the arch a camber, and that's how the town
got its name. The way down into the glen was rough going
through thick woods, but it was possible in those days. However, the rock arch must have weakened over the years and
eventually it cracked through and dumped tons of broken
boulders onto the woods, killing the trees and burying
everything, so that the way to the glen was completely
blocked."

As I looked down at all that mass of jagged rocks and thrust-
ing tree stumps, I could almost hear the roar in my ears as
everything collapsed. Then I realized it was only the bulldozer again, just out of sight beyond the top of all that rubble.

"So nobody can get down there anymore?" I asked.

"That isn't quite true. I understand there's some means of
getting down—a way that Will Horst knew, of course. But the
townspeople don't tell strangers where it is. I'm sure every
kid around here knows the secret, though, and I'll bet there's
hardly a boy or a girl growing up in Camberhills who doesn't
take his turn at going down there to hunt for the money from
the Putney Bank."

"Then why hasn't it been found?"

Mr. Myrick shrugged. "I can think of several reasons. One
might be that there are thousands of hiding places down in
the glen, and even reaching up into this avalanche of rock.
Though I don't imagine Horst and Boyd would have done
much climbing into all this, because it's unsafe and really
makes a very good barrier."

I could see that it certainly did. All sorts of wild growth had spread over the pile of broken rocks — creeping vines and scrubby brush — so that it was covered by a treacherous carpet and footing could never be sure. Uphill from all this mass the noisy bulldozer seemed to be nibbling away at the edge of it, and now and then I could hear men shouting.

Mr. Myrick went on. "Because that stuff down there rolls and shifts and could crush a man if he started a rockslide, I suspect that the robbers picked a good hiding place among the goblins. A really good place might escape treasure hunters forever."

I looked down toward the goblin rocks in disappointment. There must be hundreds of those little figures. Uphill the bulldozer seemed to have bitten off a mouthful of rock to send it crashing away in another spot.

"What's happening up there?" I asked.

Mr. Myrick gave me his wry smile. "What you're hearing is the Battle of Camberhills. Mr. Davidson, the selectman I mentioned, wants to cut a road down through the pass into the glen, though there are those who want to stop him."

Building a road through this river of rock would take a long while, and I was interested in getting down there now.

"What other reasons are there for the money not being found?" I asked.

"Perhaps there are two," Mr. Myrick said. "Some treasure hunter may have found the stuff long ago and skipped out, never saying a word about it. The other possibility is that either Horst or Boyd slipped the word to some relative or friend who came here knowing where to look and got it out."

I could see all my foolish dreams about being a real-life heroine collapsing just as thoroughly as the rock arch had collapsed.

"Of course," said Mr. Myrick, "there's still the curious matter of the map." He started briskly back to the car and I flew after him, my attention thoroughly caught.

"Map? What map?" I cried.

He grinned and waved me into the front seat. "It's a funny thing about treasure hunt fever, isn't it? It's more contagious than measles and it can last a lot longer."

He started the car and drove on along the top of the hill, with me impatient beside him. The cliffs and glen vanished at once, hidden by thick pinewoods, so you'd never have guessed they were there if you didn't know. I waited impatiently until he got ready to talk about the map. I had a feeling he was teasing me again, so I didn't say another word.

After a while he answered me. "You'll find the map in the Camberhills library carefully locked away under glass. Your Great-uncle Will apparently drew it to keep a record of where the money was hidden. His daughter found it among his papers after he died. She sent it to old Andrew Putney, probably in the hope of making up for the crime her father had committed in his youth."

I stared at Mr. Myrick. "But then why—?"

"Oddly enough, nobody could ever figure out what the map meant," he said. "Grownups and kids have been poring over it for years, and no one has come up with an answer. People have been poking around in Goblin Glen, with and without the help of that map ever since the robbery. Without the slightest success. So by this time the adults in Camberhills are inclined to think the money is no longer there. A small point of fact that no one with romance in his soul will ever accept."

Exactly what that meant, I wasn't sure, but Mr. Myrick had turned the car onto a narrow gravel side road, and I began to pay attention to where we were going. WHITE OWL ROAD, a sign said, and I liked the sound of that. In a few minutes the car turned again—this time onto a driveway that led into an open space behind the huge white house I had seen from Main Street down below.

"Welcome to Goblin Acres!" Mr. Myrick said.

His eyes were twinkling and I stared at him suspiciously. "That's not its real name?"

"It is now," he told me. "My daughter Florida has named it, and it's fitting enough, don't you think—being so close to the glen?"

I got out of the car and stood looking in surprise at the house. From below I had known it had to be big. But seen close up—it was enormous! It spread out wide on both sides of the front door, with the biggest veranda I had ever seen running across its face. And above, there were gables and dormers, peaked roofs, and high balconies, all thrown together in a wonderful jumble.

Mr. Myrick was staring at the house and his thin face wore a look of mingled despair and admiration.

"Sometimes I think people are like that too," he said. "All made up of bits and pieces thrown together in a jumble. Some of the pieces are exactly right, and some of them never fit together and always fight with the rest. Never mind—just look at the house as a whole and enjoy it. And take the bits one at a time so they don't confuse you too much. Let's go in, Trina. It doesn't sound as though the rest of the family is home, so I'll have to do the honors."

The moment we crossed the veranda and stepped inside, a dog with a high, snappish bark began to sound off furiously. Mr. Myrick shouted at him to be quiet, but I heard his toenails clattering against the wood of a door at the end of the hall as he tried to get to us.

Inside, the house was as interesting as it was outside. I knew Mrs. Myrick ran a small private antique business, picking things up for her friends—so I wasn't surprised to be met by a somewhat chipped marble copy of the *Venus de Milo* the minute I stepped into the front hall. This Venus wasn't much like the pictures I'd seen in my schoolbooks because she wore a stylish-looking blond wig, drippy earrings made of cardboard, and a pink scarf around her shoulders—to keep away the drafts?

Mr. Myrick noticed my astonishment and shook his head sadly. "The poor thing had to play a countess in a performance last night," he said. "It was Florida's idea to dress her up, and I must say it's not an improvement. Your room is upstairs, Trina. Come along and I'll show you."

Florida was beginning to sound rather interesting and I grew more and more anxious to meet her.

Mr. Myrick had brought my suitcase in from the car and I followed him up wide, uncarpeted wooden stairs that led to a small landing and took a turn to the floor above.

"Half the rooms aren't furnished," he said, "and I don't suppose they ever will be. But you might say that they are at least populated."

I could see what he meant as we followed a long hall that ran the width of the house, with rooms on both sides. Some of the doors stood open, and all sorts of things had been piled into each room—lamps and baby carriages, an old-fashioned iron stove, a butter churn, a slightly bent lamppost. Mrs. Myrick had been busy collecting. Then we came to a closed door at the end of the hall and Mr. Myrick pushed it open, indicating this was my room.

I was relieved to see that this one really looked like a bed-room—and a very nice one. The furniture was old-fashioned and cheerful, with a bright rag rug on the floor, and a patch-work quilt on the bed. There was even a rocking chair with a yellow cushion. But I paid hardly any attention to all this because of the windows. This room was across the end of the house and there were windows on three sides. I ran from one to another, looking out toward the front drive, then at a wide stretch of grass at the side, and finally to the back windows, where there was a wonderful view.

This was the part of the house that could be seen from downtown, and not only could I see the clustered houses of Camberhills far below, with Main Street cutting through them, but I could look out at rolling hills beyond, with woods and roads and little ponds making up the wide landscape. I was so entranced that I hardly heard Mr. Myrick speaking behind me.

"Make yourself comfortable," he said. "That meeting must be breaking up by now, so the family should be home soon. Neighbors are giving them a lift back. And—Trina . . ."

Something odd in his voice made me look around. He stood in the doorway watching me and there was no twinkle in his eyes.

"About Tex and Florida"—he went on. "They're both good kids, but sometimes they take a bit of getting used to. Florida has some pretty weird notions at times and she's a very imaginative girl. Just bear with her and I think you'll come to be good friends."

I stared at him blankly, not understanding what he was trying to tell me. It seemed almost like a warning. Then he gave me his wide, kind smile and went off toward the stairs.

I stepped to the door and closed it softly behind him. I wanted a little time alone to get used to my new room, and think about what he seemed to be telling me.

As I swung the door shut, I jumped in surprise because for a second I thought someone was standing there behind it. Then I realized that the gentleman in the corner was only a marble bust on a pedestal. He had a long curving nose and blank white marble eyes, and there was a wreath of laurel carved about his head. At the base of the bust a name had been spelled out, not in marble, but in marking ink. The letters spelled the name PETRARCH. I remembered vaguely that Petrarch was an Italian poet who had lived a long time ago, but I couldn't understand why he was in my room. Or perhaps it was the other way around and he didn't understand why I was in his room.

"I'm sorry, Mr. Petrarch," I said, "but maybe they'll find you a new place tomorrow. This is a pretty big house."

He went on thinking his own thoughts, looking dignified and tragic. I was half tempted to hang one of my blouses over his face, but that seemed too fanciful, so I turned my back on him and went about the business of unpacking and settling in.

I set my suitcase on the bed, opened it, and began to take out my things. The room had a little closet with a few hangers on a rack. I made trips back and forth to hang up the clothes I had brought, the floor creaking under me at every step. When I got to the last hanger, I found a piece of paper attached to it, and brought it out into the light to see what it was.

The paper had been torn from a school pad and something had been drawn on it rather crudely in purple marking ink. It was the sort of picture a five-year-old might draw—a cross-eyed face with straight-up purple hair and a long thin neck. The mouth was drawn in a single downward curve, and underneath the ugly little face were three black letters: U G H. Did that mean "Ugh"!—and if so, "Ugh" *what?*

The thing made no sense and I wadded it up and threw it into a wastebasket. When my dresses and blouses were all hung up as neatly as though Mother were watching me, I opened a drawer in the old-fashioned bureau to put away the rest of my things and another of those peculiar faces looked up at me from inside the drawer. This one had its mouth open, showing a jagged row of angry-looking sharks' teeth, and hor-rid, cauliflower ears, all drawn in bright green. Underneath was a longer row of letters. Again I held the paper up to the light and read the phrase aloud: "GO AWAY."

There was no doubting the meaning of the words this time, but I couldn't see why they should be intended for me. People don't treat guests like that. I was beginning to feel a little an-noyed, and this time I didn't throw the paper away. I laid it on the bed and began looking around the room to see if I could find any more.

I could—and did! There was another one in the bottom drawer of the bureau, one under the cushion on the rocking chair, one under the pillow of my bed, and one inside the bed when I turned down the covers. Perhaps there were more that I didn't find—but these were enough. All the drawings were of horrible little faces done in purple and red and green, and each one had a different message: HORSTS AREN'T WANTED HERE, MIND YOUR OWN BUSINESS, BEAT IT, and, finally: LOOK OUT.

By the time I had gathered together as many as I could find, my heart was thumping furiously, and when I glimpsed myself in the bureau mirror I saw that my face had grown as bright as my hair. This wouldn't do at all. I took the sheets of paper and put them into a writing case in my bag, closed it, and shoved it into a far corner of the closet. Then I got out my hairbrush and began to brush my long straight red hair as hard as I could.

While electricity crackled and tangles pulled at my scalp, I tried to think what this was all about, and what I had better do. My first idea was to take my collection of ugly little pictures straight to Mr. Myrick and ask him what they were. But I put

that notion out of my head quickly. Mr. Myrick was a writer, and I knew I mustn't disturb him any more than I had to. Dad had warned me about that. Mr. Myrick had already taken part of his workday to meet me at the airport and drive me home. Besides, it would be no way to make friends with Florida and Tex if I ran straightaway to their father with tales about them. For the same reason, I didn't think I would go to Mrs. Myrick either. This was something I had to handle myself. But how?

Why should Tex and Florida Myrick not want me here? Why should they care whether or not my mother's maiden name was Horst? They didn't belong to Camberhills, or have any connection with the people Mr. Myrick had spoken of who had been hurt by the bank robbery. So what were they up to?

As I brushed my hair and stared at the little I could see of myself in the high mirror, a wicked sort of light came into my eyes, and I knew I had found a way to handle this. I have very green eyes—like the villainess often has in stories I've read—and when I get the right look in them I can make them sort of glittery and narrow and dangerous. Florida and Tex had better look out for themselves. Trina Corey was no unimaginative adversary. *Adversary!* That was a lovely word. And if Florida had an imagination, so did I. I knew a way to puzzle them without stirring anything up.

The dog began to bark again and there was the sound of car doors slamming. With a solid thump I set down my hairbrush and scooted for the door. I liked it better with the door open. Old Mr. Petrarch was hidden in his corner, and I could hear everything that was going on downstairs, even though the hall was a long one.

Mr. Myrick was telling them I was here. Mrs. Myrick was exclaiming over the way *Venus de Milo* hadn't been returned to normal, the dog was yapping and whining, a boy's voice was saying, "Down, Chipper, down, Chipper!"loudly. But as far as I could tell there wasn't a single peep out of Florida Myrick. If she was there with the others, she wasn't making a sound. I was about to tiptoe back into my room, when Mrs. Myrick came part way up the stairs and called to me.

"Trina? Are you there, Trina? Do come down and join us. We've brought ice cream and cookies. Come and have some, dear."

I looked at my watch which had been a present last Christmas, and saw that it was after five o'clock — which seemed an odd hour to be having ice cream and cookies. But I didn't know the Myricks then. They seemed to have meals when and if Mrs. Myrick thought about it.

So I went downstairs and followed in the direction of voices, walking through more halls and a huge, empty dining room in the first-floor wing of the house. Eventually a swinging door led me to the kitchen.

It was a big room, with everything as old-fashioned as in the pictures of country houses I had seen in books. The sink enamel was scarred with rusty brown cracks and the drainboard was wooden, but there was a new refrigerator and an electric stove.

The Myricks were all there, and so was their noisy little tan-and-white terrier, yapping around underfoot. Mrs. Myrick saw me at the door and came to give me a warm hug and a kiss on the cheek. She is a large woman, as I've already said — a lot bigger than Mr. Myrick. Her face is pretty and cheerful, and she has very blue eyes that often look a little vague, as if she's trying to think of several different things at the same time. As soon as she stopped hugging me, I turned to have a good look at Tex and Florida.

Tex is almost as tall as his father. He has light brown hair, and light brown eyes. And he has muscles. The athletic type, undoubtedly, unlike his father, who looks as though a good game of ping-pong would wear him out. When his mother introduced us, Tex seemed cautious, though not unfriendly — as though he wasn't sure how I was going to turn out, and didn't mean to commit himself ahead of time. I knew right away that it was Florida I must count on for trouble. Somehow I was already sure Tex hadn't drawn those faces. But Florida was burrowing in the refrigerator and she didn't turn around until her mother spoke to her.

Even though she is two months younger than I am, she's a

lot bigger, and I knew it was going to be the same old thing—
with me always smaller than everyone else. Like the little dog
dashing around under our feet, trying to call attention to himself. Except that I didn't mean to be like that with Florida. I
wouldn't beg for her friendship, no matter what.

She turned around when her mother spoke, and I was surprised at how pretty she was. A little on the fat side—but
awfully pretty. Even prettier than her mother. She had a smile
that flashed at me in a surprisingly friendly way as she came
over and shook my hand properly—which was more than Tex
had done.

"Hello, Trina," she said. "It's nice that you've come to
visit us."

So who had put those marking-ink faces in my room? Who
else was there to do such a thing? I stood there shaking her
hand stupidly, not knowing what to think. Then I noticed her
eyes—and I had the answer. Her mouth was smiling at me,
but her eyes were as cold as ice cubes, and I knew the very
words she was thinking: Beat it! Go away! Look out! Ugh!

Beads of clammy perspiration started out on my forehead,
and I pulled my hand away. This was a mean sort of girl. She
was putting on an act to fool her parents, but she didn't care
whether she fooled me. She only wanted me to go away—and
I had better find out why. I had better find out soon, or I was
going to have a pretty miserable summer. By the way she was
looking at me I knew she meant to give me a bad time every
chance she got, and it was all I could manage to keep my
temper on a leash.

At least I had a plan, and I didn't mean to let her know she
had disturbed me in any way. That, in fact, was part of my
plan.

3 *Stay Away from the Woods!*

MR. AND MRS. MYRICK beamed at their daughter because she was being so polite, and their daughter beamed at me.
All the while, in my suitcase upstairs, those ugly little messages
were hiding and I knew perfectly well that she had put them
there.

We sat down at a round kitchen table covered with a blue-
and-white plastic cloth, and we ate chocolate-chip ice cream
and ginger cookies. And while we ate, Chipper, the little
mongrel terrier, watched us hopefully, thumping his tail. No
one paid much attention to him, so when I had a chance I
slipped him a bite of cookie, thus making him my friend forever.

Mrs. Myrick was talking enthusiastically about the meeting
downtown. Sometimes Tex added a few words, but Florida
said hardly anything. That seemed rather strange, as I didn't
think she was a shy girl. I could feel her watching me, but I
couldn't catch her at it. Every time I looked at her, I was in
time to see her glance away. Since I couldn't get her to look
straight at me, I couldn't turn on my wicked green glitter and
let her know just how deadly I felt toward her. Something was
going on behind those big blue eyes of hers and I had to find
out why she was so set against me.

Mrs. Myrick began to talk about the town's Mr. Davidson,
who was apparently young and energetic, and bent on putting
Camberhills back on the map of America where he felt it belonged.

"He's going to build a road down into Goblin Glen and open it to the public," Mrs. Myrick said. "The Folk Festival is just the beginning of all he's planning. He hopes to bring in enough money to complete the road and make Camberhills one of the most interesting little towns in New Hampshire."

Mr. Myrick choked on a cookie. "Camberhills already has everything it needs! Beauty, quiet, its own legends and traditions. A road through the cut we can do without! What can a road like that possibly accomplish?"

Tex grinned at his father. "It's for treasure hunters."

His mother nodded her complete agreement. "We're going to get Camberhills advertised through the New Hampshire Chamber of Commerce, and we're going to tell the whole story of the bank robbery and Goblin Glen, and about how the money has never been found. Once the road goes through we'll invite tourists to come in and have the fun of a free treasure hunt."

As I listened, it seemed to me like a perfectly awful plan. Why couldn't they just let old Will Horst and what he had done be forgotten except by the people who lived here?

At her words, Mr. Myrick yelped as though a bee had stung him. "That," he said, slapping his hand down on the table so hard our dishes jumped, "is the most revolting idea I've ever heard. Repulsive is the word for it. Anyway, Andrew Putney, whose bank was robbed, still owns the land the glen occupies, doesn't he? And he'll never let the town have it for such a purpose."

"That is one of the things Mr. Davidson has to work out," Mrs. Myrick said cheerfully, not at all disturbed by her husband's disapproval. "Somehow we must persuade old Mr. Putney either to sell or lease the land to the town. It isn't worth a thing to him, you know. Not with all those rocks and cliffs. Hardly anyone believes the money is still there after all these years, so it isn't as if he needed to protect the glen."

"So Camberhills, led by this idiot of a selectman, means to perpetrate a fraud?" Mr. Myrick snapped. "There isn't any treasure, but you're going to invite the public in to search, so it will visit Camberhills and spend money here?"

His lean face wore an outraged expression, but his wife only smiled at him sweetly.

"We don't know for sure that the money isn't there. Besides, even without the treasure, the glen is an attractive place to use for sightseers, just the way other scenic places are used—caves and falls and so on."

Tex broke in earnestly. "I'll bet Galvin Sewell will try to keep his great-grandfather from letting the selectman use the land. Old Mr. Putney listens to him and nobody can do anything about Galvin. He's the town's juvenile delinquent."

"Oh, come now!" Mrs. Myrick said. "Let's not call names."

Florida stopped watching me in that sneaky way long enough to support her brother's words. "He has already had two fights and he's painted letters on the town hall fence since we've been here. I don't know what he'll do when he finds out there's a Horst back in town."

This time she looked directly at me, but I was too startled to do anything but blink.

Mrs. Myrick said, "Now, dear," and looked at me too—a bit uneasily, as if something about me worried her.

"Are you going to tell Galvin she's a Horst?" Tex asked pointedly of his sister. "Otherwise, how would he know?"

Florida had thick blond hair that fluffed out around her face, and when she tossed her head pertly, tendrils of it danced around her face. I fingered the straight red strand that hung over my shoulder and gave it a rebellious tug.

"No one is going to tell anyone anything," Mrs. Myrick said firmly. "You've both promised and I'm sure Trina won't mention it around town. It's better not to. I've really been surprised to see how much feeling lingers on about what happened. The minute people get onto the subject of the robbery you can sense how bitter they still are. We want to be happy here and stay away from controversy. New Englanders can be slow about accepting strangers, but everyone has been nice to us, so don't let's rock the boat."

So that was why she felt uneasy about me. I could feel myself getting prickly with resentment and Mr. Myrick noticed. He put down his spoon to reach out and pat my hand.

"I suppose you know, Trina, that your great-grandfather, Fred Horst, once owned a livery stable and blacksmith shop on Main Street? The old place has been turned into a garage, but it's still there. You can see it when you go downtown."

"Just the same," Mrs. Myrick went on, "it's best to say nothing about Trina's connection with the Horsts."

Tex and Florida looked at each other in an odd, secretive way and I saw Tex move his head slightly in a direction away from the table, as if he gave a signal. But it was a signal to which his sister did not respond. She turned away and spoke to her mother.

"When are the Buddy Brothers coming? Have you heard from them yet?"

"They're driving up tomorrow," Mrs. Myrick said. "The young man named Joe phoned me today. They aren't sure when they'll arrive, but they want to be here ahead of the festival in order to rehearse in the town hall."

"Rehearse!" Mr. Myrick said. "You mean they need practice to make noises like that?"

Florida paid no attention. Her face had taken on a dreamy look that I understood very well.

"Imagine!" she said softly. "Al and Joe Buddy are coming right here to stay in this house! I'll get to see them, and talk to them. Maybe Al will give me a lock of his hair."

Mr. Myrick choked again, though there were no cookies left. "May I ask why you favor—what's his name?—Al? Why not Joe? What's the difference?"

Florida blinked and came out of her trance. "Well, Joe too, of course. But it's Al the girls like best. He has such a wonderful smile and he looks as though he really knows that you're out there watching him. He has a darling face and—"

"A darling face!" Mr. Myrick echoed, sounding quite ill.

Even though I agreed with Florida about Al, I felt contrary by this time and I wanted her to know it.

"I like Joe best," I said, sounding grumpy and abrupt. "He's certainly the best singer."

Everyone stared at me. Mr. Myrick continued to look pained, and Tex made an "Ugh" face. Florida looked pitying, as though I couldn't possibly know what I was talking about.

"Joe can only sing on key," she said scornfully. "What Al can do with his voice is fantastic."

Mrs. Myrick smiled at her fondly. "I can remember Frankie boy," she said. "Sinatra wasn't so good-looking, but all of us were mad about him in those days."

"At least Sinatra can sing," Mr. Myrick said.

Florida wrinkled up her short little nose. "Oh, Dad—he's an old man!"

"And so will these Buddy boys be, one of these days," her father said. "And *your* daughter, my Florida Key, will be mooning about someone else and she'll look at you as if you were hopelessly dated when you mention these Buddys. I doubt if there'll be a soul alive who remembers these two long-haired guitar players. In fact, I suspect they'll be forgotten by next summer."

"Oh, Dad!" Florida said in acute pain, and this time I had to agree with her. Being old was something very distant and far away that would surely never happen to us. Time crept along minute by minute and it took a long time to grow up, let alone get old.

Mr. Myrick muttered to himself and suddenly Florida looked at him with interest.

"Listen! Dad's making up a jangle. Say it out loud, Dad."

Mr. Myrick gave her his wry grin and did as she asked.

> "In youth a man will often bear
>   What in age he'd seldom wear.
> I doubt that I will ever care
>   To see a Beatle with gray hair."

Everyone laughed, and Mr. Myrick winked at me.

"This is a jangling family, you know. Not jingles, but jangles. There's a difference. A sort of calypso without music. They can rhyme any old way and they don't have to scan."

"They have to make a comment on the social scene," said Florida primly.

Mrs. Myrick had been sitting with her eyes closed and her lips moving. "All right—I've got one for you. Listen!

"If Sinatra caused Mom's heart to flutter,
Let's not condemn her squealing daughter."

The game sounded like fun, but before I could try thinking up a jangle of my own, Tex broke in abruptly.

"When do we have dinner?" he asked. "I'm hungry."

His mother looked at a red kitchen clock hanging on the wall and cried out in astonishment. "Oh, goodness! I thought it was much earlier. I forgot all about dinner. I'm afraid we'll have to have it late again. Why don't you all run along and let me have the kitchen to myself. By the time I catch up, you'll have room to eat something more."

Tex and Florida slipped away from the table and ran for the door so quickly that they must have had some prearranged signal. Mr. Myrick said he would try to get back to his type-writer for a while, and Mrs. Myrick began rattling pots and pans around the sink. Everyone seemed to forget me for the moment, so I slipped away too, and stole softly up the stairs after Tex and Florida.

When I reached the top step, I looked cautiously down the hall and was just in time to see the two of them pop through the door of my room and close it behind them. My first impulse was to go after them, fling open the door dramatically and demand what they were doing in there. But I could almost hear Dad's voice telling me to think, so I stopped at the head of the stairs and tried to figure things out.

I had an idea of what they were up to. They would be checking to see if I'd found those ugly little warnings — since I hadn't said a word about them. Of course that was my strategy. I thought it might throw them off balance if the pictures disappeared and I didn't even mention them. This was still the best plan, so I turned around and went softly downstairs past Venus in her blond wig, and out the front door.

Chipper was racing around the driveway and when he saw me he came bounding over. At least he didn't care whether or not I was a Horst. I bent to pat him and he got terribly excited and began to play a game. He would race away toward a path that led off through the woods, and then he'd bound back to me, yapping and leaping. Clearly he wanted me to follow that path.

I walked around the side of the house and then paused because there was an opening in the trees on the downhill side and I found I was looking west toward the sunset. We were high enough, so I could see low hills rolling away, with the shine of sunset pink water off to the left of the town. Already the town itself was almost lost in the shadow of its own hills, but the sky beyond was gold and pink and amethyst. I stood there for a few minutes just feeling it. The air seemed so clean and clear and as I watched the whole western sky began to flame as if it were on fire. I wondered how Goblin Glen must look now, buried so deeply between its cliffs, with all those little rock men leaning in the same direction as if they had to hurry-hurry-hurry to reach some hidden place before the dark night came down and caught them there. I shivered pleasantly at the eerie thought.

Chipper yapped at my heels so impatiently that I gave in to him and walked toward the opening in the woods. I wouldn't go far, since I didn't care to be caught in among the trees after the sun went down. But at least I would have a look and discover what direction the path took. It seemed as though it might very well curl around in the direction of the cliffs above the glen. The little dog yelped his pleasure and bounded ahead of me, but before I had taken more than a few steps into the woods, someone called my name from the direction of the house.

I looked back, but though Goblin Acres stood full in the fire of the sunset, with its windows burning red, I couldn't see anyone for a moment. Then a voice shouted, "Trina, don't go in there!" and I looked up to see Florida leaning on the windowsill of an upstairs room, waving at me forbiddingly. For a moment I felt obstinate enough to turn my back on her and follow Chipper in among the trees. But it might be even more interesting to find out why she didn't want me to take this path, and I went back across the yard and stood below her window.

Tex leaned out beside his sister and they both looked down

at me without the slightest friendliness.

"The path through the woods is private," Florida said. "You're not supposed to go in there."

"What will happen to me if I do?" I called back.

This time Tex answered. "You might fall off the cliffs. It's dangerous to go walking in that direction unless you know the way. Sometimes the rock crumbles."

I stood staring up at him, saying nothing. Why should it be necessary to walk on crumbling rock? If other people could learn the way in, maybe I could too. But I wouldn't say this to them. The path could wait until tomorrow when it was light. Something else had waited long enough and I'd better see to it.

"I want to talk to you," I said, and I hurried back into the house and up the stairs.

The long upper hall was growing dim and no one had turned on a light. I couldn't tell which of the many rooms Tex and Florida were in, except that they must be down the hall from my own end room and on the woods side of the house. I walked slowly along the uncarpeted hall, looking through one door after another. In one room I thought someone watched me, but when I found a light switch and turned it on, I saw the face was only a scowling Japanese mask hanging on a wall. The room was just another storage place for things that Mrs. Myrick had not yet found a spot for around the house.

When I came opposite what might be the right door, I found that it was closed. I rapped on the wood and called, but there was no sound from inside. When I turned the knob the door wouldn't open. A queer silence had settled over everything with the approach of sunset. Only from the distant kitchen could I hear a banging of pots and pans, where Mrs. Myrick was getting a rather noisy supper. In the farthest wing of the house a typewriter clattered, marking Hugh Myrick's presence. But close around me everything was as quiet as though the house held its breath, waiting. I had a feeling of eyes watching me, of someone standing very still—on guard against me.

A minute of that gave me goose bumps and I ran down the hall to my room to let myself through the door. Once more Mr. Petrarch frightened me, standing like a ghost in his corner behind the door, but I found the switch for the overhead light and turned him back to cold marble. There was no key, so I could not lock my door, but at least I felt safer when it was closed. One thing I settled right away. There were two pillows on the bed and I only needed one. So I took off the extra pillowcase and hung it over the marble face of the bust on the pedestal. I felt better as soon as those blank marble eyes stopped following me around the room.

When Mr. P. was put to sleep like a bird on its perch, I pulled my suitcase from the closet and opened it. The ugly drawings were there where I had put them, tucked into the leather writing case Mother had given me to encourage letter writing.

I didn't feel like writing letters just now, however. I felt unwanted and let down, and even a little frightened. No one had ever treated me so hatefully before, and I found myself wishing for our apartment back in New York, where everything was in beautiful order and the windows overlooked Riverside Drive. I missed the voice of the city. This was the first time I'd ever truly realized that New York had a voice — a sort of distant roar made up of car and truck and people sounds — busy sounds. Here it was too still, and somehow the very stillness made me miss my mother and father. In such quiet there was a loneliness that hurt like an aching tooth.

Then, quite suddenly, it wasn't quiet anymore. Someone was whispering outside my door. The English language is full of "s" sounds, and when people whisper there's a sort of hissing, so you know right away what is happening. I tiptoed to the door and put my ear against the panel. I couldn't hear the words because the voices were so low, but there was an argument going on. I turned the doorknob softly and jerked open the door.

Florida and Tex stood just outside. Tex was scowling, while Florida's face was bright and excited. When the door flew open they froze for a minute, staring at me in surprise.

Florida spoke first. "We know what you're here for. We know what you want. Why don't you go back home to New York and mind your own business?"

I took a few steps backward into the room, feeling smaller than ever beside those two. Tex was almost as big as his father, and while Florida wasn't nearly as large as her mother, she was huge beside me, and there was a kind of wild, excited look about her, so I couldn't tell what she might do.

"Don't be scared," Tex said to me. The scowl had apparently been for his sister and the look he gave me was reasonably kind. He seemed to recognize how I might feel better than his sister did.

I had backed as far as the end of the bed, with Florida following practically on my toes. I glittered at her as hard as I could, making my green eyes narrow, and clenching my fists close to my body to show her that I'd fight if she tried anything.

She laughed suddenly and stepped back from me. "You look like Chipper when he gets ready to defend our house against something six times his size."

That didn't help me to feel any better. I always hate it when bigger kids make fun of me because I'm small. But before I could say anything, Tex asked a direct question.

"What did you do with those silly pictures Florry hid around your room?" he asked.

Here was my chance. "What pictures?" I said innocently and was glad to see Florida blink.

Tex looked at me with interest. "You see?" he said to his sister. "I told you the whole thing was foolish. She isn't a baby to be frightened by tricks like that."

Florida shrugged and took a few steps around the room. "How could I know till I tried? Now I'll have to think of something else."

It was time to have this out with Florida Myrick. "Why must you think of ways to frighten me?" I demanded. "I only wanted to be friends when I came this afternoon. And I don't scare easily. So why are you acting like this?"

"We're acting like this because I have a nutty sister," Tex explained, suddenly looking like his father as he grinned at me. "She gets notions and talks me into them. I ought to know better. Come off it, Florry. You can't keep this up all summer."

His sister paid no attention. In her turn around the room

she paused beside the statue of Petrarch with the pillowcase over his head.

"What's this for?" she asked.

"I don't care for his company," I said. "Perhaps somebody can move him out tomorrow."

"But then you won't have anybody to talk to," Florida said. "I have Julius Caesar in my room, and Mom has Shakespeare in a cupboard in the kitchen and Vergil in the bedroom. Even Dad has a marble friend to complain to when his writing sticks — Edgar Allan Poe."

I must have looked at her as if she had grown two heads, because Tex burst out laughing.

"Mom has a thing about chipped old marble busts that nobody wants," he said. "Dad wishes she'd collect something lightweight like postage stamps, but she feels sorry for them and she likes to have them around. Of course we don't know for sure if this one is Petrarch. Florry put down his name." Tex pulled off the pillowcase to indicate the inked-in marking. "He could be anybody, I suppose."

"And do you have a — a marble friend?" I asked him.

When Tex groaned it sounded just like his father. "As if I would!" He beckoned to Florida. "Come along and let Trina alone. This idea isn't going to work and you might as well forget about it."

"Only if she promises to stay out of the woods," Florida said.

Everything seemed suddenly clear. "I suppose you want me to stay out of the woods because that's the secret way into Goblin Glen? Is that what you mean? Are you afraid I might go down there and find all that money?"

The two exchanged a look of meaning, and this time I knew Tex was on his sister's side against me.

"Being a Horst, maybe you know something nobody else does," he pointed out. "Maybe old Will left some information in the family so his relatives could come back here and find the money one of these days."

This idea was so silly that I could only glare at them both angrily.

"*Do* you know something?" Florida asked softly, leaning close to look right into my face as though she meant to hypnotize the truth right out of me.

"If you believe that, you *are* nutty!" I cried. "Why are you so interested in that lost bank money? You haven't any right to it anyway."

Again there was a look exchanged between them, but this time neither answered me. It was as if they were in firm agreement on one thing at least. They turned around abruptly and walked out of my room. I was glad to see them go.

The moment they were through the door I slammed it shut behind them. Slammed it hard because it felt good to release my indignation. There can be something satisfying about a good hard door slam. Of course afterward someone always comes hurrying to tell me not to be noisy. But this house was so big that though the echoes went ringing down the hallway, no one came to scold. Tex had tossed the pillowcase over a chair and I didn't bother to cover Mr. Petrarch again. He was only a chipped old marble bust, after all.

I went to kneel before the window, with my arms on the sill. The sky was darkening and there was only a thin strip of pink left across the west, with the gray edging in, to narrow it. Pine trees on the steep slope below the house whispered in the evening breeze, and fireflies danced among darkening tree trunks. The world smelled of pine needles that had been warming in the sun all day, and everything seemed calm and peaceful out there, with only a few birds chirping as they settled for the night, and the insect chorus just beginning.

In spite of the loneliness, it was so beautiful I couldn't help feeling a little better. What Florida Myrick held against me was an imaginary sort of thing. I ought to understand another girl with an imagination because I had one myself. She was acting out make-believe in her mind and as soon as she found out how unreal her ideas were she would surely get over what was bothering her. It was hard to believe that Tex and Florida could really think that I had come here with some secret knowledge of the lost bank money. Though I had to admit they were right about my wanting to find it.

As for Al Buddy—Florida could have him as far as I was concerned. I liked Joe better, I decided. He was the dark, serious, rather homely one of the two. When I saw them on television I always felt as though I wanted to comfort him for not being as gay and good-looking and popular as his brother. I was sure he was a better singer, though he never got much of a break, because it was usually Al who did the singing part, while Joe filled in and mostly played his guitar to accompany his brother.

Thinking about the Buddy Brothers helped quite a lot. In spite of the growing darkness outdoors and the hatefulness indoors, I began to perk up with anticipation. Tomorrow was going to be fun, no matter what the Myricks did. The path through the woods invited me to explore it, and I meant to accept the invitation. There was a treasure map in the library to be studied, and I had made no promise not to look for the long lost money. In fact, it would be a stroke of just fate if *I* could be the one to find it. I could imagine myself triumphantly presenting all that money to the town and thus making up for everything Great-uncle Will had done. When the town got through thanking me, no one would ever hold anything against the name of Horst. Even Great-grandfather Fred would be proud of me if he were alive.

It was a wonderful dream and I went right on dreaming it up to the moment when Mrs. Myrick sent Tex to call me downstairs for supper. Of course I hadn't the faintest inkling then of the strange things that were about to happen in Camberhills. Real-life things—not the made-up imaginings of two girls named Trina and Florida, but happenings that were a whole lot more desperate and dangerous, and concerned people I hadn't even met as yet.

4 *Danger in the Glen*

THE next morning right after breakfast, Mr. Myrick went off to his end of the house to spend a few uninterrupted hours on his latest spy story. Florida and I helped Mrs. Myrick with the dishes, while Tex went outdoors with Chipper at his heels. Afterward, Mrs. Myrick asked if we'd like to assist in getting things ready for the Buddy Brothers' arrival.

Of course I was eager to do anything I could for Al and Joe, so she didn't have to coax. I had only to think of all the girls my age who would jump at this chance — and I was ready to get down on my knees and scrub floors.

Florida was equally willing, but I wondered what sort of plans she was cooking up. She was very pretty this morning, with her plump face and fluffy golden hair — not at all like a girl who would do mean things. But I watched her warily, not daring to trust her. I knew now that any friendliness she showed toward me was for her parents' benefit, and that when we were alone she could turn hateful in a minute. Tex seemed a lot more sensible and kind, yet both were together when it came to their own plans for finding the lost money. That, at least, was clear.

Mrs. Myrick led the way into a small foyer in the opposite wing of the house from the part we occupied. Here a door opened into a huge room with a very old, very beautiful Oriental rug covering most of the parquet floor. Furniture, hidden under white dust covers, stood all around, and a chandelier that dripped crystals hung overhead. Everything was shadowy and dim until Mrs. Myrick moved from window to tall window, flinging back green brocade draperies. Then sunlight slanted into the great room to set the chandelier to gleaming with rainbow lights, and I could see a beautiful rose-and-white marble fireplace, with the portrait of a man hanging over it.

Florida dashed about snatching off dust covers so that the fine old furniture could be seen, and Mrs. Myrick stood in the middle of the room, misty-eyed and dreamy.

"This is the first time I've really seen this wing," she said. "Rosalie Sewell rented us the rest of the house under the condition that the downstairs rooms of this wing be left just as they used to be. It's strange, isn't it, to think that this is the Putney house? Andrew Putney lived here in the days when he was wealthy and very well known in the State of New Hampshire. But when the bank failed after the robbery, he had to move out of this house. No one wanted to buy it because it is so big, so from time to time the family has rented it to others. These few rooms have always been left just as they were in Mr. Putney's time. Now and then Rosalie comes up here to give the rooms a good cleaning and she likes to wander around in here, though she never lived in the house herself. She wants to help with the festival, so she was happy to have the Buddys stay here. Rosalie Sewell is a very fine person. Almost all her life she has looked after old Mr. Putney, and after her parents died she practically raised her young brother, Galvin."

At mention of Galvin's name, Florida snorted and made a face. "Galvin is the enemy," she said.

"Oh, Florry—stop that!" her mother cried. "Trina, you'll like Rosalie. At present she has a job looking after our little Camberhills library."

I stopped staring around the beautiful room and stared at Mrs. Myrick instead. "You mean the town librarian is Andrew Putney's great-granddaughter?" The thought made me uncomfortable. I spend a lot of time in libraries, and to think that the librarian here would be a person who would surely despise all the Horsts made me squirm. More and more I was beginning to feel that I didn't want anyone outside of the Myricks to know about my family connection.

Mrs. Myrick must have caught my expression. "Of course we won't tell her," she said quickly. "We won't tell anyone. About your great-uncle being Will Horst, I mean."

This was what I wanted, yet at the same time it didn't make me feel much better. I had never before been in a position where I was supposed to be ashamed of a member of my family. Will Horst wasn't my fault and I hated all this need for secrecy.

"Old Mr. Putney's portrait is over the mantel," Mrs. Myrick went on. "It was painted when he was a fairly young man, though he was already enormously successful. Rosalie feels it should be given to a museum eventually, but for the time being it pleases the old man to have it here in his former home."

I looked at the painting with new interest, and Florida came to stand beside me.

The man in the picture had a strong, bold, assured look. His eyes seemed to look directly out at me from the picture, challenging me a little, yet in a friendly way.

"I think he must have liked people," I said.

"If he did, then it must have been all the worse for him to be the cause of so many people losing their savings," Florida said.

I looked at Andrew Putney's firm mouth, just barely smiling, and at the strongly marked cleft of his chin. This was a young man. Now he was very old and I hated to think of the lifelong injury Will Horst had done him.

Mrs. Myrick went to get the vacuum cleaner and I glanced at Florida curiously.

"Why should you and Tex want to find that money?" I asked.

For once I took her by surprise. She blinked and answered before she had time to think.

"It doesn't belong to anybody anymore. And we want it for Dad. All those people who lost their money in the bank must be gone, and it wouldn't do Andrew Putney any good now. But Dad needs it terribly, and—oh, never mind!" She broke off and walked away from me.

We could hear her mother coming and I knew that Florida was already sorry for telling me so much.

While Mrs. Myrick got ready to vacuum the frayed but still

handsome draperies, she went on to explain a little more about these rooms. This had once been a guest suite because the Putneys had enjoyed having visitors from out of town. More than once the governor of New Hampshire had stayed in these very rooms. Here guests could have their own parlor, two bedrooms, and a bath. Which made it a very fine place for Al and Joe to stay—better than they were probably used to. As everyone knew, the Buddy Brothers had grown up in a poor part of New York, and never had much of anything until they became popular and began to make scads of money with their records and appearances. I had a sudden hope that they would appreciate these rooms and do them no harm. But that seemed a disloyal thought and I put it quickly out of my mind.

As we went to work setting everything in order, I began to see how much Mrs. Myrick loved all the fine old things in these rooms. That chair over there with the shield back was real Hepplewhite, she said, and that drop leaf table with the lyre base was early Duncan Phyfe—a beautiful design of his best period.

I hoped to get better acquainted with Florida Myrick while we worked. I was curious over what she'd said about Galvin Sewell being an "enemy," and I also wanted to find out what she meant by her odd remark that her father needed money "terribly." I know from Dad that writers often spend years earning very little even when their books get published—unless they become popular. But the Myricks didn't seem to be in any special need. Anyway, I had no chance with Florida because she managed to work in one of the bedrooms when I was in the parlor, and the other way around, clearly avoiding me, so we couldn't get together.

When we were finally finished, I felt as though I had spent the morning cleaning a museum, and I was ready to go outdoors and move around in the air for a while before lunchtime. I hadn't forgotten that path in the woods and I kept hoping for a chance to follow it when nobody would notice what I was doing. An opportunity came my way almost at once.

Mrs. Myrick sent Florida upstairs to tidy her room, and since I had done mine early in the morning, I was free to do whatever I liked. If Florida had been my friend, I might have helped her, but I knew she didn't want me around. Tex was still off somewhere on his own, but when I went out the front door I found that Chipper had come home alone. The minute the little dog saw me he perked up his pointed ears and wiggled all over with pleasure. Then he bounded off toward the path. This certainly must be his favorite walk. No one seemed to be paying me any attention, and I ran after him, straight into the woods.

The path curved and twisted, following its natural course along the hillside. The automobile road was somewhere uphill on my right, but it couldn't be seen because of the trees and all the thick underbrush. Green sunlight slanted through the branches and the warm scent of pine needles made the air smell like Christmas. I was wearing jeans this morning and they were fine for walking in the woods.

The house was quickly lost from sight behind us and everything seemed secret and lonely out here. Chipper appeared to know where he was going, however. He would dash ahead along the path, wait for me to catch up with him, and then dash off again. I remembered what Tex had said about falling off the cliffs, or stepping on crumbling rock, and I walked with care, even though the way seemed perfectly safe and solid.

Then, just as I was relaxing a bit, thinking he had only tried to frighten me, the path curved around a big oak tree and ended in a small clearing. Now I could see the danger—and it was real. The place where the path stopped seemed to be near the rocky edge of the cliffs, though a six-foot-high wall of rock blocked my view into the glen. Straight ahead, however, the way was open and I could see the cliffs running on clear to the great platform rock where Mr. Myrick had taken me yesterday. That way might very well be dangerous.

I called anxiously to Chipper and he bounded out of thick brush that grew below the rocky wall. There seemed to be no place to go from here, and since I couldn't see over the mound of rock into the glen, I decided I'd go back to the house. The walk was a big disappointment. Somehow I had expected a more interesting adventure, considering the way Tex and

Florida had been so anxious to warn me away.

Chipper yapped at me again, and once more dived into the brush. I called him back and he returned, looking as disappointed with me as a dog can look. Apparently he wanted to show me something more.

The third time he disappeared I got down on my hands and knees and looked into the rough brush into which he kept disappearing. There seemed to be a sort of crawl space here that couldn't be seen when a person was standing. The grass was worn down as though more than a small dog had come this way.

My feeling of adventure surged back. "Go ahead and show me!" I called to Chipper, and I crawled after him into the low opening in the brush. My long hair caught on twigs and even got under my hands on the ground, giving me a nasty tug, but I managed somehow. The crawl space took a turn or two and then opened out upon a rocky area nearer the edge of the cliff. But here the rock ramparts rose in pinnacles higher than my head and there was no place where I could see over, and no place to go from here.

Except that Chipper was once more gone! I called and whistled, but he didn't reappear.

Brush and tall weeds grew all around the little clearing, making of it a pleasantly secret place. All I could see around me were rocks and brush and trees—and overhead the wide blue sky. A hawk was wheeling up there and I watched it for a while, until Chipper popped up at my feet to bark at me again.

"Where did you go?" I said. "What are you trying to tell me?"

This time I watched him closely, and when he ducked behind a thick bush that seemed to grow at the very edge of the rocky wall, I bent down and looked under it. Chipper was gone—and the only place he could have disappeared into was a small cave that seemed to open close to the ground. The wall of rock rose above it and I knew there must be nothing beyond but a drop-off down into the glen. I wished I could see over, but I didn't want to climb those high pinnacles of rock.

Chipper poked his head out of the small cave and spoke to me as clearly as he could with little yaps and whines and wriggles. "It's all right," he was saying. "Just follow me."

I had never been in a cave before and I wasn't sure I wanted to go into one alone. Perhaps I would just poke my head into the opening and see what it was like before I returned to the house.

But when I knelt on the rough rock and looked into the opening, I could see that dim light seeped into it somewhere ahead, so it wasn't completely dark. I had to go through the opening on my hands and knees, but once I was inside I found I was in a cave large enough for me to stand up inside its walls. Light filtered through from a slit high in the rock ceiling, and while it was an indirect light, I could at least see the brown rock walls all about me.

Others had been here too. Near one curving wall stood a cardboard carton with some picnic things in it. Not food, but paper plates, plastic spoons, and an old aluminum cooking pan that looked as though it had been blackened over a fire. Next to the carton lay several rough gunnysacks—old potato sacks, neatly folded but empty. I wondered what they were for. To sit on, perhaps?

Clearly this was the secret which Tex and Florida wanted to keep to themselves and I couldn't blame them. If I had found a private cave, I wouldn't want anyone else coming into it either.

Chipper was still dashing delightedly around inside the hollow, pleased that he had persuaded me to follow him, but now he dived through another opening in the rock wall, then backed out to wag his tail at me furiously. Apparently there was more for me to see.

"All right," I said, giving in. "Show me."

He almost grinned at me, dived once more into the opening —and simply vanished. Vanished so completely that all I knew was that he went downward deep into the earth. Before he disappeared I saw his waggling hind end and stubby tail— and then that was all. From somewhere below I could hear scrabbling sounds coming back to me as though his toenails clicked and slipped over hard rock.

Once more I knelt and put my head gingerly into a dark opening. I found that I was at the top end of a slanting, rocky tunnel that seemed to plunge in a long slide down into the hillside. At the far end a bright circle of sunlight gleamed, so I knew the tunnel must come out in the open. Down there was Goblin Glen!

Chipper was already out and I could hear his barking, magnified to a roar by the echoing rock of the tunnel. If I ventured headfirst into this opening, as Chipper had done, I would be able to slide straight down the hill. It wasn't a pleasant idea and at first I didn't want to try it.

I stood up and looked around the larger cave, trying to figure out a way to get down more easily. Suddenly I thought of the gunnysacking, and I picked up one of the folded bags and shook it out. A fine brown rock dust floated from it, and I knew what it was for.

The idea was strange and a little frightening, but since others

had done this before me, it must be all right. I couldn't bear
the thought of leaving without finding out where this tunnel
went. Oh, I knew well enough—but I wanted to prove it. I
wanted to see for myself.

Carefully I folded the sack and placed the thick, rough pad
it made just inside the lip of the tunnel. Then I crawled onto
it, facedown. Here the space was fairly level, but I could see
that if I propelled myself along with my hands, I would reach
the smooth, slippery floor of the slanting part. Aeons ago water
must have worn its way through here, rushing downhill, eating
out this softer core of rock, polishing the stone almost smooth
—polishing it into a slippery slide.

Chipper barked entreatingly at the far end and I couldn't dis-
appoint him. I took a deep breath and shoved off. Under my
stomach the gunnysacking made a sled, and I found that if
I raised my arms, pointing them ahead as if I were diving, I
could travel smoothly enough. I wasn't centered quite right
on the sacking, though, because my knees were taking a batter-
ing behind me. But once I'd started there was nothing to do
but slide straight down that slanting floor as though I rode a
roller coaster into the depths of the earth. It was scary, but
fun. And the trip down went too fast for me to get really frightened. I'd have been a lot more scared if I had stuck somewhere
along the way.

I didn't stick. I plunged down the slide and shot out of the
lower end, stopping quickly as soon as I hit a level place of
grassy earth. Chipper was waiting for me and when I landed
on my stomach, he came over and licked my face enthusiastically. I shoved him away and scrambled up. My knees were
stinging a little, but my jeans had helped protect them. My
sneakers were brown with earth and so were my jeans, but
I had no time to worry about getting dirty. This was the secret
passageway into Goblin Glen!

From where I stood there was only a weed-grown bank of
earth to descend—rather steep, but easy to get down. When I
reached the foot of it, I would be out among all those leaning
rock figures. Behind me rose the straight walls of the cliff I had
tunneled through, and I saw that the pinnacles weren't nearly

as high above the glen at this point as other cliffs farther along. So the tunnel hadn't needed to be terribly long and steep, even though the cliffs went straight up and couldn't be climbed.

The entire glen was open to the sky, and the bright glare of noon poured down upon it. There were no shadows at this time of day, yet somehow the place had a strange, grim darkness about it. The rocks were a dull brown—almost black, so they didn't reflect the sun, and some of the little men seemed to have turned their heads to look at me.

There must be hundreds of them down there, I thought, all grouped in individual clumps. It was as if communities of goblins had huddled together for protection. What were they afraid of? I wondered. The skin at the back of my neck prickled, though the sun was hot on my head. This really was a melancholy place—a place that would be just right for the enactment of some crime. And there had been a crime—the hiding of that lost money.

Now, however, the idea of finding anything that had been hidden here years ago seemed ridiculous. Where would I begin to look? Where could I possibly look that others had not looked better before me? My dream of being the town heroine and making up for what Will Horst had done went trickling weakly away like any other magnificent make-believe. Just the same, I knew that I must come back here another time. I must walk out among all those hurrying little men and see the place for myself. After all, they were only rock and I could bring Chipper with me for company. But I didn't want to do this now. I would have to get used to being in Goblin Glen first.

I picked up the gunnysack and started back to the tunnel opening. There I got down on my knees and looked into what seemed like an impossibly tall, slanting chimney. Much too steep a chimney to be easily climbed.

The thought hit me suddenly and with full force, leaving me weak in the knees. What had I done—plunging down the hillside without a thought for how I was to return? I looked at Chipper and he seemed less happy now. He rubbed his head against my knee and whined.

"How do we get back?" I asked him. "How on earth can we get back to the top?"

He was a bright little dog and he seemed to understand my worry. He ran to the opening of the tunnel and barked loudly. I could tell that he was worried too. His slippery toe nails and pads would be fine for sliding down—but they would never help him when it came to getting back up.

Overhead the sun went behind a cloud. It was only a fluffy summer cloud, but the moment the brightness vanished, the whole glen blackened. Everything turned into one big shadow, through which little goblin men scurried for their lives—yet never moved from one place.

Or did they move when it was dark? Did they hurry around at night, or when the sun went behind a cloud? It seemed to me that there was some sort of movement down here—a shifting of shadow thickness, as though something crept among the goblin figures.

The thought frightened me so badly that I crawled into the tunnel and tried to pull myself frantically upward over the rocky floor. Behind me Chipper yelped in real terror, and even if I hadn't kept sliding back as fast as I crawled up, I couldn't have left him behind. How was I to get out of this place? No one had noticed where I went, and it might be days before Tex and Florida came here again. If they ever did come this far, considering that there seemed to be no easy way back.

What an utter, stupid tenderfoot I had been! I knew from stories I had read that the first rule in exploring any strange place is to let someone know where you're going.

I stood up and looked fearfully around the glen once more. There! Something moved among the rocks. There was no mistake about it this time. Some animal, perhaps? Something that crept among one of the central groupings of little men? But surely there were no dangerous wild animals in this part of New Hampshire. Chipper growled low in his throat and I leaned over to put a hand on his back to quiet him. His short hair bristled and I knew whatever was down there was not friendly.

Anything was better than this creepy feeling of something

watching me and I shouted loudly, so that echoes went crack-
ing around the cliffs like pistol shots repeating themselves.

"Who's there?" I shouted. "Who is it? Who's there?"

Very slowly, a boy stood up tall among the goblin men,
staring at me over their heads. He looked as though he might
be about fourteen—taller than Tex—a thin, lanky boy, with a
shock of thick brown hair that fell over one eyebrow, and eyes
so dark and fierce that I could almost feel the heat of his
anger clear down the glen. As he came toward me, the grim
set of his mouth and the way his long jaw was tightly clenched
told me he was furious. So furious that I wanted to turn and
run away from his anger.

But there was no place to which I could run. I could only
stand there and watch him come toward me, wondering what
was going to happen now.

5 *In Pursuit of a Map*

WHO are you?" the boy demanded rudely as he drew near. "What are you doing down here?"

I stood my ground, feeling upset because he had frightened me so badly, and also because I had put myself into a foolish jam. At least this boy could tell me how to get out of this place. He certainly couldn't leave me here, no matter how angry he was.

"My name is Trina Corey," I said. "I'm staying with the Myricks. Who are you?"

He didn't bother to answer, but scrambled up the steep, grassy bank, while Chipper growled fiercely and stayed close to me. When the boy reached us, he stopped and stared at me again, his dark brows scowling.

"So you're with *them!*" he said. "You're with those two kids who have come to live at the Putney house! Haven't they told you you're not supposed to come down here?"

"They haven't told me anything," I said. "Chipper showed me the way. Nobody even knows I'm here."

"Well, I know!" he snapped. "This is private property. You could be arrested for trespassing."

Being pint-size, I hate it all the more when anyone tries to bully me — so now I pushed the hair back out of my eyes and braced myself to stand up to this boy.

"Then what are you doing here?" I challenged him.

He looked a little surprised — as most people do when some-one small shows spunk. And that makes me mad too. As if what goes on inside a person—I mean things like spirit and courage—have anything to do with whether anyone is little or big.

"My great-grandfather owns this land," he said. "We don't want strangers coming down here."

So this boy was Galvin Sewell.

"What are you going to do when the town builds a road into it?" I asked. "How are you going to keep strangers out then?"

His face turned an angry red. "There won't be any road. They've started it, but it can't be finished without Great-grandfather Andrew's permission. And that won't be given. He has already promised me."

I remembered that Florida Myrick had called this boy "the enemy," and I could understand why. But I didn't see how he could keep guard on a place that had drawn treasure seekers all through the years. Part of what he said was bluff, I was sure, but I was just as glad that this angry boy didn't know my great-uncle had been Will Horst.

By this time all I wanted was to go back to the house, so I didn't argue with him. "How do I get out of here?" I asked. "I came down through the tunnel, but I can't climb up again. Is there another way out?"

He looked at me scornfully, pityingly. "You mean you haven't any more sense than to come down that slide without thinking about how to get back up?"

I could feel my own face turning red, and the fight seeped out of me because now his attack was justified.

"It was pretty stupid," I admitted. "Can you tell me what to do now?"

He walked gruffly past me to the opening in the hillside and then beckoned. "Look inside and tell me what you see. Look inside—and use your head!"

When I knelt and looked into the opening everything was so dark that I couldn't see for a few seconds. As soon as my eyes adjusted, I found myself once more looking straight up a long slide that was nothing but rock. There were no hand or toe holds—nothing.

"At the sides!" Galvin said impatiently behind me. "Look

at the sides — low down. Put your hand in."

I reached wonderingly along the slanting rock floor at one side and closed my fingers upon something rough and snaky — a length of rope. When I tugged, the rope grew taut in my hand and I knew it must run clear to the top — secured to something solid up there.

"There's a rope on the other side too," Galvin said. "If you take hold with both hands you can pull yourself to the top. Keep your feet astraddle of the floor and you'll find there are enough rough gutter grooves at each side so you can almost walk up, with the ropes to keep you from sliding back."

I pushed myself out into sunlight and found Chipper dancing excitedly about my feet. "How do I get him up?"

"He doesn't belong down here in the first place," Galvin said, "but I'll take care of him. You go ahead of me."

He picked up gunnysacking and small dog and bundled them under one arm. Chipper made no objection. Whether he approved or not, he seemed to know what was expected of him.

Now that Galvin was directing a project, he sounded less angry. Though I supposed he was doing this mainly to get me back to the top and be rid of me.

I crawled into the cave and took hold of the ropes with both hands. As soon as I was well inside I found I could get my feet into grooves in the rock on either side of the floor and walk myself up. In no time at all we were on our way up — not very comfortably, but at least without much trouble. I couldn't slide back, braced like this. Behind me I could feel Galvin tugging at the ropes and knew he would have traveled up a lot faster than I could, even managing Chipper, simply because he was used to this manner of passage.

About halfway up I called to him that I wanted to rest, and we stopped there in the dark tunnel. It was queer to be deep inside the earth with that one little porthole of light ahead of us at the top, and another one at the bottom. The tunnel wasn't a tight fit around us, but it wasn't very spacious either, so there could be no standing up or turning around. Once in, you had to keep going in whatever direction you happened to be pointed.

While we rested I asked the boy behind me who had figured this out.

"I don't know exactly," he said. "It was long before my time. My great-grandfather told me about this way down when I was small. I guess people who grew up here always knew about the tunnel, and after the natural rock arch fell in, some-body figured out this way of getting up and back. When the ropes begin to wear they get replaced, so it's safe enough."

"They must have taken a lot of wear during the last forty years," I said, thinking of the hunting that had gone on for the lost money.

"Let's get going," Galvin said gruffly and I could have bitten my tongue for irritating him so that he stopped talking.

My arms were aching by the time we neared the top, but I gritted my teeth and kept on, not wanting to let him know. When we reached the upper cave, Chipper was first out in the sunlight, and this time he was so pleased to reach the top that he dashed off for home without waiting for me. I crept out behind the brush that hid the cave and stood up, stretching my arms and rubbing them.

Galvin crawled after me and when he stood up I thought what a bean pole he was, scowling at me from his height.

"You're pretty lucky I was there," he said. "It gets cold in the glen when night comes. It's not a comfortable place to be."

I could believe him. "Thank you for rescuing me," I said, and crept beneath the brush to get back to the path. He was behind me right away, and when we reached the open he scrambled ahead and barred my way.

"What did you mean?" he asked. "What did you mean back there—what you said about the wear the ropes must have had in the last forty years?"

I wouldn't let him stare me down, so I stood with my feet apart and stared right back at him. After all, what had hap-pened in the glen was hardly any secret.

"Everybody knows about the bank holdup," I said. "And an awful lot of people must have hunted for that money. Why do you suppose they haven't found it? Mrs. Myrick says there's a map in the library that's supposed to tell where it was hidden."

He looked so mad I thought he would explode. "Just you stay out of here!" he snapped. "And you tell those nosy Myrick kids to stay out too. It's bad enough that you're all up there in my great-grandfather's house, without your going down in the glen too!"

The way he looked, with that lock of dark hair falling over one eye and his mouth set and grim, I began to feel uncomfortable again. There are times when it's better to retreat than to take a stand. I ducked past him and scurried as fast as I could toward the house. Because I'm light and quick, I can outrun most boys, but he didn't bother to come after me. There was no sound of thudding feet on the path behind me, and I took the twists and turns among the pines as fast as I could go, stopping out of breath just before the path opened onto the Putney house grounds. There I peered cautiously from behind the trunk of an oak tree before I stepped onto the grass.

Luckily I had stopped before I came into view, because Florida was sitting on the side steps of the veranda watching the opening to the path. I backed away still more to be sure I was out of sight, and then I looked down at myself.

It was a good thing I did. The front of my jeans was brown with rock dust, and so were my sneakers. There was dirt on my blouse and probably on my face as well as on my hands. Higher up the hill, on the road, I heard a car going by — and that gave me an idea. If I could get to the road through the woods, perhaps I could come back to the house from another direction, as though I'd been circling around. For the present, at least, I wanted to keep where I'd been a secret from Florida and Tex.

I left the path and struggled through more underbrush, hoping I wasn't stamping through poison ivy. When I reached the pine trees, the going was easier because intertwining branches overhead had killed off everything in the shade underneath, and there was space to move about. Here, well out of sight of the house, I went to work, dusting myself off as best I could. Fortunately I wasn't really dirty. The rock dust brushed off pretty well. I stamped my sneakers hard on the ground, and scrubbed at my face with my handkerchief. Then I climbed the

rest of the way to White Owl Road and walked along its grassy edge until I came to the Putney driveway. As I followed it in I began to whistle in order to announce the direction of my approach.

Florida heard me and jumped up to look, thoroughly suspicious. "Where have you been?" she demanded. "Mom's waiting lunch for you."

I waved my hand in the general direction of the woods and answered as airily as I could. "Oh, I followed your forbidden path to find out where it went. But it doesn't go much of anyplace, does it? So afterward I cut through the woods back to the road and came home." All of this was perfectly true, except for leaving out a few things.

"And it took you all that time?" she asked, staring at me hard.

Something felt sore in my right palm and I realized I must have a blister from the rope. I didn't dare look to see. For some reason it seemed awfully important to keep one jump ahead of Florida and Tex about what I knew.

"I wasn't walking all the time," I told her. "I'm sorry if I'm late. I'll hurry and wash and be right down."

Before she could ask any more questions or get too close to me, I dashed into the house and ran for the stairs, then along the upper hallway to the bathroom. There I had a look at the white puff of blister on my palm, and I washed my hands and face, dusted myself some more, and did a lot of fast thinking.

Two separate notions were running through my head. I remembered Galvin Sewell's anger about the road the town wanted to build into the glen, and I felt I understood why it worried him. If this was to happen, then time was running out. Before many more months, anyone at all could drive right into that secret place. Anyone could come in and hunt for lost treasure. So if Galvin was ever to accomplish what no one else had managed to do in the last forty years, then he would have to do it fast. Somehow he must never have given up hope —and if he had not, then perhaps all the grown-ups were wrong and the money was still hidden in Goblin Glen.

Somehow I wished that Galvin would let me help him look for it. Not that I could do any better than he had. It was only that I wished I could make up for the dreadful thing Will Horst had done. But Galvin had already lumped me with Florida and Tex, and he probably knew very well what they were up to on their own. Besides, if he knew that my mother's name was Horst, he would be more set against me than ever. He wouldn't be the sort to give me a chance. All I wanted was to keep this shameful fact secret from anyone who didn't already know.

My second notion had to do with the map Mrs. Myrick said was on display in the library. To have a look at that map was my next goal. It didn't make any sense that Will Horst had set everything down in a detailed plan—supposedly so he could return and find the money—and then have the map not work. I simply had to find out why.

After I had taken several swipes at my hair with a brush, it looked fairly smooth, though there was no time to comb out the tangles. I went down to the big kitchen where the Myricks were already having lunch.

"Sit down and help yourself, Trina," Mrs. Myrick said cheerfully. "We didn't wait any longer."

They were all making their own sandwiches. Cold meat, two different kinds of bread, peanut butter, jelly, and a big tray of assorted cheeses had been set out. I sat down and went willingly to work. Goodness knows, I was hungry enough after all that sliding through tunnels.

Mr. Myrick seemed a little absentminded, and when anyone spoke to him, he would start as if it was a great surprise to find other people in the same room. The third time it happened, his wife smiled at me, explaining.

"Hugh really isn't here, you know. He's off somewhere in Spyland worrying about the problems of his characters. They're more real to him than we are right now. He'll come back to us at dinnertime."

Mr. Myrick heard her and made a horrible face. "Spyland! That's as bad as Buddy Brothers. As a matter of fact, my present story is set in Athens, so that's where I'm spending my time. And if you don't mind, I'll take this sandwich and a wedge of cheese and get back to work."

I think he was off to Athens again before he even reached the door. Mrs. Myrick looked after him fondly.

"If only he could drop those spy stories and take the time to do a really important book," she said. "The sort of book Trina's father believes he can write. Perhaps if he finishes two or three more quick ones for the paperbacks, he can take time — a year or two, if necessary — to write something good."

Tex and Florida exchanged a look with meaning in it, and something stirred in my thoughts. All that matter of their father needing money — was this why?

"Not," Mrs. Myrick went on, "that we need a great deal of money. That's one reason why we've come here to a small town. It's so much cheaper than a city. If we can get ahead a little with some popular books, then Hugh can do something that really matters."

Neither Tex nor Florida said anything, nor did they look at each other again, but I had a strong feeling that a message was flying between them. A great deal of money — at least for that day—had been involved in the Camberhills bank robbery, as Mother had told me. Banks all around the country were shaky at the time, and Mr. Putney had been afraid of a run on his bank, should all the people in the area suddenly decide to take out their savings. So he had brought in a large amount of cash from outside to take care of anything that might happen. That was what gave Will Horst and Burt Boyd the idea of picking up a windfall—which was exactly what they did. This had not only wiped out the depositors who lost all their savings, but it had also left Mr. Putney hopelessly in debt to the friends who had loaned him the cash. Because of all this, my heart certainly wasn't touched by sympathy for Mr. Myrick, who seemed happy enough with what he was doing, and not at all in need of money that didn't belong to him. Florida, as her brother said, was a little nutty.

Right after lunch, Tex announced that he was going fishing with another boy, and Mrs. Myrick said she must pick up some groceries in town before the Buddys arrived. She invited Florida and me to go downtown with her, but Florida shook her head.

"Not me! Al and Joe might come while we were away. Someone besides Dad has to stay here to welcome them."

Her face shone at the very thought and I was tempted to stay too, so as not to miss the big moment of their arrival. On the other hand, they might not get here until late in the afternoon, and this was a wonderful chance for me to do a few things I had in mind downtown. Such as taking a look at that map.

So Mrs. Myrick and I drove off, leaving Florida to change her dress and get herself fixed up for the great occasion. I would do the same as soon as I got home, but now there wasn't time to change from my dusty jeans, and I got into the station wagon beside Mrs. Myrick, hair tangles and all. Of course I should have known better!

This time we didn't go the long way around to get a view of Goblin Glen, and the drive to town took hardly more than five minutes. The way ran downhill to the "Y" in the road, leading into Main Street. Mrs. Myrick found a place to park and left me on my own. She had quite a lot to do, she said, so I could take my time. Whoever got back to the car first could wait for the other.

I remembered where the library was and I headed for it straightaway. Before I went in I took time to look through the glass and I saw that the librarian was again working at the desk. Now I knew who she was — Rosalie Sewell, Galvin's sister, the great-granddaughter of Andrew Putney.

She was absorbed in her work and didn't notice me peering in at the glass. In the back of the room were several rows of bookstacks, while up in front was a round wooden table with chairs set about it, a rack for magazines, and some display shelves for new books. It was the plainest library I had ever seen, but that didn't matter because it's the books that make the inside of any library wonderful. Just the look of them invited me, and I had to remind myself that taking out books wasn't my main reason for coming here today.

The door stood open. Inside, an electric fan was buzzing, though it wasn't doing very much good. The afternoon sun poured in the front windows, and there were no other windows, except perhaps behind a partition at the back, so it was pretty warm inside. The floor was bare, but my sneakers made no noise, and I was at Miss Sewell's elbow before she looked up and saw me.

At once her blue eyes lighted and I liked her right away. She wasn't at all like her angry young brother. She had light brown hair and she hadn't teased it into any high-in-the-air style. It fell just below her ears and turned up perkily at the ends. She had a mouth that looked made for smiling, and there was a deep cleft in her chin that reminded me of Andrew Putney's chin in the portrait back at the house.

"Hello," she said. "You're new in town, aren't you?"

I smiled back at her. "I'm visiting the Myricks for the summer," I told her, waiting to see how she would take this.

She picked the matter up without hesitation. "Then you're Trina Corey from New York. Mrs. Myrick said you were coming. It will be nice for Florida to have company. I'm Rosalie Sewell, the librarian."

She hadn't mentioned that the Putney house belonged to her great-grandfather, and I liked her all the more for that. She wouldn't be touchy and sensitive like her brother.

At the back of the room there was a sound as though someone slid books along a shelf, but I couldn't see who was there. The aisles between the stacks were narrow in order to fit in as many rows of bookshelves as possible, and I could see only into those directly opposite.

I stood looking around the long room with interest and my eye was caught by a black, fat-bellied stove with a big stovepipe rising from it and disappearing into the wall overhead. I had never seen a stove like that except in pictures and it fascinated me. Books were stacked upon it now, as though it were in use mainly as a table.

Miss Sewell saw my interest. "We don't use the old stove anymore," she said. "We have steam heat, but we keep it because it once belonged to the grocery store that used to occupy this space. We've kept the store clock too, and the scale the storekeeper used to weigh out groceries on. Young people today don't have much opportunity to see what an old-fashioned country store used to be like."

The big round-faced clock still ticked away in its place high on the wall, and it still appeared to be telling the right time. Miss Sewell moved about the library, pointing things out to me, and I followed her eagerly, watching for the one thing I had come to see.

"In the wintertime," she went on, "we get a strong smell of codfish over there where the codfish barrel used to stand, and sometimes I catch the aroma of ghostly pickles."

I moved on to a case that stood against one wall and looked into it at the books on display behind the glass, and at a square of paper beside them with markings on it in ink that had faded to brown. The paper was tacked to a piece of cardboard and set at a tilt so that it could be clearly viewed. Even without the lettering at the top that said GOBLIN GLEN, I would have known that this was the famous map.

Again Miss Sewell noticed my interest. "Not every library has a real treasure map on display," she said, not sounding disturbed about it as Galvin had. "Perhaps you've heard the story of the Camberhills bank robbery?"

I nodded, not daring to say anything, not wanting her to guess how interested I was in this very map—yet feeling a little guilty at the same time. I didn't want to pretend with Miss Rosalie Sewell.

"One of the bank robbers actually drew that plan," she went on. "It was found among his things after his death, and his daughter sent it to my great-grandfather years ago."

"I've heard about that," I said, and all of a sudden I felt so uncomfortable and deceitful that I could hardly bear it. Miss Sewell was being kind and friendly, but I wondered just how kind and friendly she would be if she knew who I was. I didn't want her to know—but I looked up into her blue eyes and found that I had to tell her.

"My mother has told me a little about what happened," I said. "My great-uncle's name was Will Horst."

Miss Sewell drew in a quick breath of surprise, while back in the stacks somebody dropped a book with a loud slam. I jumped at the sound and looked in that direction. Then I saw what I had done. Galvin Sewell came out of a rear aisle and walked toward me, his eyes dark and fierce. Apparently he had been there all the time, hiding from me among the books.

"So that's who you are!" he snapped. "So that's why you were snooping around down in the glen! Well, let me tell you—"

His sister put a quick hand on his arm. "Wait a minute, Galvin. It's not Trina's fault if—"

"Not her fault!" Galvin echoed. "Not her fault that she headed down to the glen as fast as she could go—knowing very well how to get there!"

"But I didn't know—" I began, and then stopped because I saw that nothing I said would do any good. This boy didn't want to believe in the truth. I knew how foolish I had been ever to think I might help him in any way. And how doubly foolish it had been to tell anyone that my great-uncle was Will Horst.

6 *The Livery Stable of Fred Horst*

I KNEW there was no use in my staying at the library any longer. Both Miss Sewell and her brother were staring at me as though they could hardly believe their eyes. Certainly I'd never be given a chance to study the map or ask questions about it now. I had spoiled everything for myself with my own quick tongue.

But Miss Sewell was not pleased with her brother, and to my surprise I saw that her warm blue eyes could snap with anger.

"That's quite enough, Galvin," she said. "I think it was honest of Trina to tell me who she is. I don't suppose she really wanted to admit it."

"She didn't tell *me*," Galvin said. "Not when I rescued her this morning and got her out of the glen."

His sister shook her head at him. "I shouldn't think she would—the way you go around snapping at people. I'm sure she wouldn't have mentioned it just now if she had known you were back there among the stacks."

I managed to find my tongue. "That's right. I would never have told your brother. He's rude and unkind and unfair and—"

Miss Sewell put one hand on my shoulder and kept her other one on Galvin's arm. "Let's think about a point we're all overlooking," she said more gently. "Something we must never forget. Trina's great-grandfather was a good and loyal friend to our great-grandfather. It's foolish to hold what one member of a family did against the rest of that family forever and ever. Did you know, Trina, that your great-grandfather had saved up some money that he wouldn't put in any bank because he was afraid of banks in those days? When Great-grandfather Andrew found himself in such desperate trouble, Fred Horst took every cent he had hidden away and gave it to Andrew Putney."

This made me feel a little better, but Galvin made a growling sound and I knew none of what his sister had said mattered to him.

"How could Fred Horst do anything else when it was his son who—" Galvin began. Then he caught his sister's look and broke off. Without another word he turned and dashed out of the library.

Inside the long room there was only the buzzing sound the fan made, and the smaller buzzing of a fly behind the front window. It seemed very hot and I was prickly with perspiration. Miss Sewell sighed and gave me a sympathetic pat on the shoulder.

"If it would do any good, I'd apologize for my brother," she said. "But unless he apologizes for himself, it won't mean anything. You came in because you'd like to see the map—is that it?"

Galvin had made me feel so guilty that I could hardly meet her eyes. I didn't think I was guilty of anything very awful, but I couldn't say a word in my own defense.

Miss Sewell took a key from her desk and unlocked the glass cabinet. Then she reached inside for the piece of cardboard with the map tacked to it.

"Come over here where there's a good light," she said, and sat down at the round table before the window, setting the cardboard before her.

Apparently it wasn't necessary to explain my interest in the map to her, or try to defend myself. Galvin's sister seemed to take my interest for granted, as if it were perfectly natural and to be expected. She had a way of making me feel easy with her, while her brother did exactly the opposite.

In spite of the fact that what must have been black ink had

faded to brown, all the markings on the paper were clear. The line of the cliffs had been drawn in, completely surrounding the glen. The stream of water was a thin thread coming from underground and disappearing underground. The place where the natural rock arch had fallen in was marked to show the rubble that blocked the original passageway. Around the curve of the cliffs, past the lookout rock, were woods and the entrance to the tunnel that burrowed under the hill, with its opening below the cliffs. The same tunnel I had gone through this morning!

But more interesting to me than anything else on the map were the small, irregular circles that had been drawn all over the glen area to represent the goblin men who gave the place its name. Of course all the hundreds of rocks in the real glen hadn't been drawn onto this small map, but there were a number of groups represented and they seemed to have names. An uneven rock that stood alone at the left of the map was marked *King of the Hills*. Three small circles on the other side were labeled *Three Blind Mice*.

I looked at Miss Sewell. "Do all the rocks down there have names?" I asked.

"Some of the more interesting groupings do, and so do some of the lone rocks," she said. "We've grown up knowing their names in this town, though I think they were given a very long time ago. Long before the robbery. Will Horst would have known about them. That's why he could draw this map so carefully. See this curving line of single-file rocks here—they're *The Marching Men*. The three smaller ones over here are *The Witch's Sons*. The Sons are such ugly little rocks that they used to frighten me when I was a child. This rather large gathering here has always been called *The Frightened Sisters*. That's because they seem to wear long garments like women's robes, and they slant all in one direction, leaning over as though they were terrified and trying to run from something."

I had seen the Sisters, I was sure. This grouping must be the very one where Galvin had been hiding while he watched me.

Bending above the map so I could examine it more closely,

I discovered what I was looking for. There in the middle of
The Frightened Sisters was a clearly marked "X." I pounced,
putting my finger on it, reading aloud the lettering underneath.

"Old Beak Nose!" I looked up at Miss Sewell. "Then this
is the place they must have hidden the money?"

Rosalie Sewell sighed. "I don't know," she said.

I stared at her, puzzled. "But doesn't this mean to show
where the money must have been hidden? Why would he put
an 'X' beside Old Beak Nose otherwise?"

She shook her head and repeated the same words, "I don't
know. Nobody knows."

This made no sense. I leaned above the map and saw that
the "X" was marked in the middle of all those fleeing women,
almost as if Old Beak Nose must be a man goblin who tried
to stand against them and was being overrun. In my mind's
eye I could imagine all those little goblin folk running madly,
with the treasure in their midst—almost as if they were trying
to run off with it and hide it forever. While the one rock called
Old Beak Nose tried to stop them.

The robbers had chosen a really difficult place where rocks
crowded in on every hand—but just the same, "X" had to
mark the exact spot, with Old Beak Nose showing where it
was.

"Why doesn't anybody know?" I asked. "Do you mean
that by the time the map was sent to Camberhills, the money
was gone? Do you mean someone tried to dig under Old Beak
Nose and didn't find anything?"

"You can't dig *under* any of those rocks," she told me. "All
the goblins are outcroppings of solid underground base rock.
You couldn't dig under them without blasting."

"Then there must be a hollow in Old Beak Nose," I said,
my excitement growing. "I should think—"

"Every single one of those figures has been searched over
since the map came to us," Miss Sewell said. "I've even had
an attack of treasure fever and gone searching myself. But
nothing has ever been found."

"Why should you search them all?" I persisted. "Why not
just around the figure called Old Beak Nose?"

"That's the biggest puzzle," she said. "You see, Trina—there isn't any goblin down there known as Beak Nose. There never has been. That's why boys and girls, and grown-ups too, have hunted thoroughly around every figure in the group, in case this was simply a name Will Horst and Burt Boyd gave to one of the figures. But no rock that looks as though it might be given such a name exists. It should be easy to identify—and it just isn't there."

I listened to what she was saying, and my eyes studied the map, but I didn't really believe in her words. I still knew that somehow *I* had to go down there and look for myself. What if some strange fate was saving *me* to be the one? What if—

Miss Sewell was watching me and a smile twinkled in her eyes. "In case you find that money, Trina, what do you plan to do with it?"

I'm sure I blushed clear to my eyebrows, but I didn't have to hesitate for an answer. I knew what I would do with it. "I'd bring it to you, of course. That's the only reason I want to find it—to make up for what someone in our family did to your family."

She touched me lightly on the shoulder again, and the smile moved down to her mouth. "I had a feeling that was what you had in mind," she said. "But I'm afraid it won't do any good, Trina. I don't want you to be disappointed. If that money was there, someone would have found it by now."

She picked up the cardboard and carried it back to its place in the glass cabinet. Then she locked the door and put the key away. I suppose my expression of disbelief and disappointment were clear to her because she tried to cheer me up by walking to the front windows and beckoning.

"Why don't you go down the street, Trina, and have a look at the garage that used to be your great-grandfather Fred's livery stable and blacksmith shop? They used to have an old sign somewhere inside that had his name on it. I don't think anyone will mind if you walk in and look around."

"I don't want to tell anyone else—" I began.

Miss Sewell nodded. "You needn't. I understand why you wanted to tell me, and I think it's to your credit. But the town doesn't need to know. There'd be a lot of staring and gossiping, and there might even be some people around small enough to be prejudiced against you. So we'll keep the matter to ourselves. Don't mind Galvin. He's upset about a number of things just now. I'm afraid he has a notion that the glen is really his personal property and that what the selectman plans will result in some stranger coming in and finding the money. Of course none of us believe that it's there any longer and Galvin can't go on behaving this way. I think it's a good idea to open the place up as a natural beauty spot and make it possible for others to visit it."

I had no idea whether such a plan was a good idea or not. Somehow it would seem nicer if caves and waterfalls and glens could just be there for people to find. But then, I suppose city people would never find them. Anyway, I understood how Galvin felt and how he must see that time was running out. Even if old Andrew Putney was saying "No" right now, he would probably give in eventually. The road had already been started and how could he stand against that?

Miss Sewell walked with me to the library door, and I thanked her and told her I would come back and get some books when I could. Then I went outside and looked for the Myrick car. Several packages had been piled in the back of the station wagon, but Mrs. Myrick was nowhere in sight, so I wandered down the street toward the garage.

It stood on a corner, just where Main Street ended as it reached the hill. The building looked like any other garage—a big cavernous place with the front of it open to the street, and gasoline pumps outside. Once there must have been stalls for horses and places where carriages and rigs were kept. Perhaps the blacksmith shop had occupied the open shed next door.

Now the place was only an unromantic garage, where two men in greasy overalls were working on cars. One car was a Ford, the other the sort of car you might expect to see around New York. A foreign make, I supposed, very low, with a long hood in front, and not an awful lot of room for passengers. The color was a bright maroon and its top was down for the summer weather. The garage man who was working on it appeared completely fascinated by it. He opened the hood as I watched and leaned over the engine as though he were looking at a case of jewels.

While his head was out of view I slipped into the garage without his noticing me and made my way along one wall. The other garage man was flat on his back beneath the Ford, so he paid no attention to me either.

Once I was inside and unnoticed, I tried to think myself back to the way the place must have looked in the past. I could almost hear the stamping of horses' hooves, and their neighing. I could practically catch the horsy smell, and the smell of leather and polish. I could imagine Great-grandfather Fred banging out a horseshoe on an anvil next door, with the sparks flying as he worked. I could even hear the hissing sound when he picked up the horseshoe with huge tongs and plunged it into a pail of water to cool it and harden the iron. I had never been in such a place in my life, but I had read stories with scenes like that, so I could make the whole thing come to life around me.

Then someone sneezed and the smell of oil and grease and machinery swept back—and I was in a modern garage again. Now I saw that a third man stood well back in a dimmer section, where hanging electric bulbs hardly reached with their light. I paid no attention to him, however, because that was the moment when I saw what I was looking for. A big sign leaned against the wall just beyond him and I had the feeling it must be the sign Miss Sewell had mentioned.

I moved toward it and saw that while it was grimy with dirt and age, the lettering could still be read: FRED HORST, LIVERY, BLACKSMITH. Right away I knew I had to get close enough to that sign to touch it. I slipped past the man who stood in the shadows and ran my hand along the top of the sign, as lost in what I was doing as the garage man was lost in working on that foreign car. My own great-grandfather had probably made this sign with his own hands and hung it outside his livery stable. His name had once been respected in this town, and I needn't apologize because I was also related to his son, Will. Miss Rosalie Sewell had helped me to understand that.

"Horst?" the man beside me said, reading the sign over my shoulder. "Isn't that the name of one of those fellows who robbed a bank here in Camberhills years ago?"

When he spoke, I looked at him for the first time. I looked and made the loudest yelping sound you ever heard. Not a squeal—a yelp. I've never been one of the squealers because that always sounds silly to me when I see it on television. All those girls leaping in their seats and yelling out those insane squeals. So I really wasn't trying it now. I was just yelping in surprise, because there I was—without being aware of it—standing about two feet away from Joe Buddy.

When I yelped, he backed away from me as though I might leap at him to snatch for a souvenir or something, the way some of the really idiot girls do. Even when he saw I wouldn't do anything, he stayed his distance, watching me warily. I tried to apologize, though I was not sure exactly what for. I felt really stunned meeting one of the Buddy Brothers all of a sudden like that, and I couldn't find the right words.

"I—I'm sorry," I said. "I didn't look at you until now because I was so interested in that sign. I didn't mean to yell when I saw you. You're Joe Buddy, aren't you?"

He backed away still more, without answering me, but his eyes went in a puzzled way from me to the sign and back again. I had plenty of time to get a good look at him and I knew I wasn't mistaken. He had to be Joe Buddy, even though he seemed different from the way he is on television. When he's playing his guitar, he's the one who wears dark glasses, and he combs his black hair down over his ears, and in a bouncy way over his forehead in front. Now he didn't look like that. The dark glasses were gone, and while his hair was long, he had brushed it well back from his forehead and behind his ears—so that I might not have recognized him at all, if I hadn't known that he was coming to town. Joe was not the handsome one of the brothers, and he looked like most any boy now. He seemed as serious as when he's performing, and I recognized his slightly crooked nose—which I'd always thought rather endearing—and he had the same big wide mouth I'd seen on television. He was dressed in an ordinary way—gray slacks

and a blue sport shirt, open at the neck.

I think he might have edged completely away from me without speaking, if the garage man hadn't yelled at him just then.

"Hey—where's your brother gone?" the man called. "I guess you'll need to leave your car here for a day or so. You want to look here and see what's wrong?"

At the sound of his voice the missing brother came through a side door and I saw Al Buddy for the first time. Al looked exactly the way he did on television. His blond hair was long all around, and he hadn't brushed it back. His eyes were a bright, sparkling blue. All the parts of his face seemed to go together, to match, as Joe's didn't. He smiled often, showing his teeth, and I'd always thought he looked like a very young and mischievous boy angel when he smiled. Sometimes a dimple showed in one cheek, but it wasn't a girlish dimple. On Al Buddy it looked exactly right.

I forgot about his rather odd brother and went right over to him and held out my hand politely. I didn't want him to get any ideas about my leaping around and screaming.

"How do you do, Mr. Buddy," I said as properly as though my mother were poking me in the back. "I'm Trina Corey, and I'm visiting the Myricks, where you're going to stay."

He gave me his wide, beautiful smile, while his brother stared at me as cautiously as ever.

"Hi, yourself," Al Buddy said, and gave my hand a quick waggle that wasn't really a shake. "You've turned up at just the right time, Trina Corey. If we have to leave our car here, we'll need to know how to get to the Myricks'."

I told him that Mrs. Myrick was downtown with her car, and was probably waiting for me now. I could run down the street and let her know—then she could pick them up with their baggage.

Al nodded. "A good idea—so run!" he said cheerfully, and turned back to the garage man. As I left I saw Joe Buddy open the trunk of the car and begin to take out suitcases and several guitars.

Mrs. Myrick was in the station wagon, wondering what had become of me, and I rushed up to her excitedly and told her the Buddy Brothers had arrived and were waiting at the garage to be picked up.

Not until after she drove down the street and the Buddy Brothers got into the station wagon, baggage and all, did I begin to take in what was happening. On the way home Al sat in front, talking cheerfully to Mrs. Myrick, while Joe and I sat behind. Joe still wasn't talking, but that was all right with me because his being quiet gave me time to think.

That was partly good, and partly bad. I remembered Florida Myrick waiting at the Putney house, hoping for a chance to welcome the Buddy Brothers all by herself. And I thought of me — driving home with them in triumph, having met them both first! But as soon as I thought of Florida, with all the time in the world to clean up and comb her hair, I remembered how I looked — with my stringy tangles, my dusty jeans, and scuffed sneakers. Both the Buddys looked neat and shiny clean. They weren't the far-out sort. Yet here I was looking like some of those messy girls I had seen in Greenwich Village in New York. Of all the bad luck! And of course it was my own fault.

I hunched in my seat and let my hair hang over my face, as though I could hide behind it. I was pretty mad at myself, and sometimes when I feel that way I want to take it out on other people. Now there wasn't anyone close enough except this dark, suspicious-looking Joe Buddy, whom I was already beginning to dislike. He had spoken to Mrs. Myrick, but after that he hadn't said a word. He sat there glowering out of the window, paying no attention to me — so that I began to feel small and unimportant all over again.

"How did you happen to know about a man named Horst who robbed a bank in Camberhills?" I asked him rather snappishly to make up for how I was feeling.

This time he looked at me, instead of out of the window, though I couldn't see his eyes because he had reached into his pocket and put on the familiar dark glasses.

"After all the publicity your town is giving this affair, why wouldn't I know?" he asked.

Al turned in the front seat and winked at me, as though he apologized for his brother's surly manner. "While we're here, maybe we'll have a look at this treasure hunt ourselves. Sounds like a good way to come into sudden money."

Mrs. Myrick said, "If the money were ever found, I'm sure it would belong to other people."

Joe Buddy made a sound that resembled a snort, but I couldn't tell what it meant, except that he liked to be unpleasant.

Al said, "Really? After all these years?" and let it go at that.

By this time we were making the turn up the hill and a few moments later we drove up before the Putney house.

Sure enough, just as I expected, Florida Myrick was out on the veranda waiting. Her blond hair was brushed glossy, and she had put on a blue dress that matched her eyes. She looked absolutely shining and clean—very pretty, even though fat. I got out of the car with my head down and crept around behind it. I didn't want anyone to notice me and compare me with Florida. But she had already seen the Buddy Brothers—and it was too late, because she had seen me too, and it was me she wanted to humiliate.

7 The Buddy Brothers

GOODNESS, Trina!" Florida said in a voice that didn't need to be that loud. "You'd better go get cleaned up for company!" Then she ran eagerly down the steps, all smiles and flashing dimples, to greet Al Buddy.

The way she was acting made me mad in a new way — mad enough to stand up straight and stop creeping around. I saw Al look at her and then at me, and I knew what he must be thinking. He started toward the house with Mrs. Myrick to meet Florida, and Joe went around to the rear of the station wagon to get out the guitars and baggage. I went with him. Anything to avoid Florida for a minute or two longer. There seemed to be several guitars — three in cases and one big wooden one without a case.

"How come so many?" I asked. "There are only two of you."

"For different sound effects," Joe said, setting things out on the grass.

"I can help carry," I offered.

Joe Buddy gave me a long stare through dark glasses and then surprised me.

"You look all right," he said gruffly. "You look fine for climbing around in the woods."

I could only blink at him, not finding anything to say for a minute or two. I had never expected a kind word from this Buddy Brother after the way he'd been acting. I found myself wondering if the difference between Joe and Al was like the difference between Florida and me. Maybe Joe behaved the way he did because he was the underdog, with Al getting all the admiration. Not that I'm really an underdog. I just won't be! But I could sympathize a little and I grinned at him.

"Florida is right," I said. "I'm a mess, and I know it. Is it O.K. if I carry one of the guitars? Let me carry the wooden one."

He picked it up and handed it to me without any argument. It was light enough, but larger than I expected, so that I took hold of it wrong and stumbled before I got my balance.

"Don't worry," I told him quickly. "I won't fall. I won't hurt it."

"You can fall on it and smash it to bits, for all I care," he said, not smiling at all. "But you'd better not, because that would upset my brother."

Al came back for his electric guitars and gave me an amused look as I turned toward the house with that awkward wooden burden in my arms. Joe brought out a suitcase, dropped it practically on his brother's toes, and then carried his own up to the veranda. Al said something unpleasant under his breath. I had seen enough to guess that the Buddy Brothers weren't really very buddy-buddy toward each other. In fact, it seemed as though some sort of quarrel was going on between them, and I wondered what it was about. At least I was getting a glimpse of what two famous people were like in real life. Somehow I hadn't expected them to be like this. Onstage and offstage were different, I supposed.

"We'll show you your rooms," Mrs. Myrick said as we climbed the veranda steps. "I think you'll be more comfortable here than in a motel."

Florida hurried to open the door from the veranda into the guest suite. I waited to let everyone go in ahead of me and then managed to stumble over the sill, so that I banged the guitar against the doorjamb. It let out a loud, chonking sound, and the strings hummed like a hive of bees.

Al looked around. "Watch it, kid," he said. "That's our bread and butter."

His brother saw I was having trouble and he set his suitcase down and took the guitar off my hands. At least he hadn't said, "You're too small to carry it." He had let me try, and I'd have managed all right if it wasn't for the door.

The big parlor shone beautifully in the afternoon light, and I was glad I'd had my share in cleaning and polishing it. Al looked around him and whistled. Joe looked too, but he didn't make a sound.

Florida flitted across the Oriental rug, her ruffles dancing and her hair abounce as she showed the way to the other rooms.

Al did not follow her at once, but stopped before the mantel and looked up at the portrait of Andrew Putney—that strong face with the cleft chin.

"Who's that?" he asked.

Mrs. Myrick explained that the painting was of Andrew Putney, a former banker in Camberhills, and that this was his house.

Al whistled increasing amazement. "You mean the same banker who got himself robbed?"

"Maybe he didn't exactly *get* himself robbed," Joe said, sounding gruff again as he walked past his brother toward where Florida waited, and I could see that Al's words and manner annoyed him.

Florida noticed only Al, however, and she looked rather gaga and silly, with her blue eyes so wide and round.

"You mean you've heard about the Camberhills robbery?" she asked Al, as though this were the most interesting news in the world.

He gave her his mischievous smile, and I had the quick feeling that he liked this sort of stupefied attention from anyone at all—even from a girl as young as Florida Myrick. Which was one reason he paid no attention to me, aside from being amused by me. Because no matter how wonderful I thought Al Buddy was on television, I wasn't going to moon at him the way Florida was doing.

"Sure, we've heard," Al answered her. "As I was telling your mother, we thought it might be fun to do a bit of treasure-hunting here ourselves."

"*You* thought it would be fun—not me," Joe said, scowling

more darkly than ever at his brother.

I wished I could see his eyes behind those dark glasses. Eyes can tell a lot about a person. Al's were smiling and friendly—practically angelic. I wondered what Joe's were like now.

Florida went completely overboard when Al smiled. "I can help you hunt!" she cried. "I know the way down to the glen."

This was so completely traitorous, even to herself, that I couldn't bear to stay and listen any longer. How awful for Galvin Sewell if there were expeditions of treasure hunters tearing up the glen, even before the road went through. And how awful for me, too—in case I could make what was called "restitution," meaning to right all the wrongs that had been done by finding that money and returning it myself.

I went out of the parlor and into the front hall of the Myricks' part of the house and ran smack into Tex Myrick coming down from upstairs. I pounced on him so fast that I must have startled him. I don't think he knew what to expect when I grabbed him by the arm with both hands, because he pulled back in alarm.

"I've got to talk to you!" I cried. "I've got to talk where nobody else will hear. Where can we go?"

He pulled his arm from my grasp and thought about this soberly for a minute. Tex was never like his sister. She acted fast and thought later—like me. He took his time and went over things in his mind before he said or did anything.

"O.K.," he said finally. "Come on up to my room."

After that big decision, he turned back up the stairs and went along the upper hall to a door that stood open. He had a large room at the front of the house, very shipshape and full of boys' things. On the far side double doors opened upon one of those turreted balconies I had seen from outside the house. The balcony looked so interesting that I went out upon it at once. There were windows all around, making it into a small room, with the roof slanting into a peak overhead. But it was the contents of the balcony that surprised me more than the room itself.

Everywhere, on wooden chairs, on window ledges, on a

table, even on the floor, were spread boxes and boxes of rocks — rocks of all sizes, shapes, and colors. I looked at Tex with new interest.

"You're a collector?" I said.

He brightened up surprisingly. "You know anything about rock-collecting?" he asked.

I had to shake my head. "Not much. Dad's company published a book for young people about minerals last year, and I was interested in reading it. But there's not much use trying to collect rocks in Manhattan. Most of the time all you'd dig up would be chunks of concrete."

"These specimens come from all over," he said. "Most of them I've found myself, but some I've swapped with other collectors. I'm going to do a lot of rock-hunting here. I've already started. Mom has a fit every time we move, because my collection keeps getting heavier. But she can't say much, the way she hangs onto those marble busts."

I hadn't heard Tex talk as much as this since I'd arrived. These rocks might be a means of making friends with him, so I let him show me a piece of gold ore from Alaska and some fool's gold from Colorado. He had a bit of turquoise from New Mexico, pieces of rose quartz from several places, and a stone embedded with bright-colored copper ores. There were even several rocks he had brought up from Goblin Glen since he had come to Camberhills.

But I couldn't let him go on like this too long, because I wanted to tell him about his sister. So when he got down on his knees to pull a box out from under a table, I began to explain about meeting the Buddy Brothers in the garage, and how his mother had brought them home. When it came to what Florida had said to Al Buddy about taking him into the glen, I must have blurted it out because I was getting mad all over again.

Tex let the box go and stood up while I was still talking. I could see that he was annoyed too. Maybe not because he hoped they would really find the money, but because Florida had gone back on everything she had said to him about keeping the way into the glen a secret.

"I know the way," I said. "Chipper showed me this morning. Galvin was there when I went down, or I might not have found my way back. How did you and Florida ever find that tunnel and learn how to get out again?"

"By following Galvin," Tex said, and went on indignantly. "After all Florry's talk about our hunting for that money to help Dad, and not letting anyone else know the secret!"

"Maybe you can stop her," I said. "There hasn't been time for her to give everything away yet."

"I'll stop her," he said. "Of all the gooney ideas—just to hand the glen over to strangers! Thanks for telling me." He regarded me earnestly for a moment. "You're O.K., Trina. I shouldn't have listened to Florry in the first place. Look—if you want to start a rock collection, I'll give you a few pieces to get you going."

I wasn't dying to collect anything right then. There were too many other things on my mind. But I tried to look interested while he picked out a handful of stones from various boxes, identifying them for me: quartz, a chunk of black granite from the glen, a piece of calcite from a cave in Kentucky—and others I forgot the names of right away. I was in a hurry to have him talk to Florida, so I cupped my hands around the stones he gave me and got away quickly. As I went down the hall to my room I heard him running downstairs and I knew this was one time when Florida wouldn't be able to boss her younger brother the way she usually did.

In my room I dumped the handful of rocks onto the bed, forgetting how gritty they might be until I saw them land on the spread. I couldn't worry about that now. Suddenly time seemed to be pressing in on me from all sides. When I stood at my window I could hear the distant sound of bulldozers over in the cut. I didn't know how long it would be before a way was opened into the glen, so that anyone who wanted to could go down there, even though the road wasn't finished. And now there was this interest Al Buddy was taking in the hunt. Of course I didn't need to worry about him too much because he wouldn't know about the library map. They could both poke around blindly down there for years without finding anything, just as everyone else had done. The map seemed to locate the treasure somewhere—if only one could be sure where. How strange that a figure called Old Beak Nose had been put down on the map—when there wasn't any such figure among the goblins, and never had been. Strange, strange, strange!

I looked at my watch. Even with the Myricks' uncertain dinner hours, there was plenty of time before it would get dark, and I simply had to go down to the glen again. By myself. I had to go out among those little black figures and stand there alone in their midst. I needed to get the *feeling* of that place.

Sometimes when I just stop thinking and feel, a wonderful idea will come to me. So now I put out of my mind all the discouraging facts and thought about the one main idea that interested me. I was the great-granddaughter of Fred Horst. Will Horst had been my great-uncle. I really ought to be the one to solve the mystery. Fate must have brought me here for this very thing.

At the back of my mind a voice tried to tell me that my father didn't think much of feeling as a substitute for thinking, and he certainly didn't believe in fate, but I wouldn't listen. In no time at all I drifted off into lovely make-believe about how I would walk up to Rosalie Sewell—of course with Galvin there too, and probably the selectman and the Buddy Brothers, to say nothing of Florida and Tex Myrick—and I would pour all that lost money into Miss Sewell's hands. Then maybe Mr. Davidson would invite me up on the platform at the Folk Festival—where I would make a gracious speech and tell them it was really nothing, and only right that I—

Somewhere in the house a door slammed, and I jumped right off that platform and back into reality. Daydreams were fun, but I had learned that they got me nowhere unless I did something about making them come true. This always meant a lot of slow, hard steps—so I might as well start taking the first of them.

This time I wrote a note before I went out, in order to let anyone who looked for me know that I had gone down to the glen. I set it on my dresser with the black chunk of granite to weight it down. Then I hurried for the stairs.

No one was around in the halls, either upstairs or down. But when I went out the front door, I found Joe Buddy playing with Chipper on the veranda. He looked at me through dark glasses and I looked back, and we both mumbled, "Hi," before I scooted down the steps and ran for the path into the woods. Behind me Chipper barked, but he stayed with Joe, and I was able to escape alone.

This time I ran most of the way through the scented pines, glad that I hadn't changed out of my jeans. But this time, before I got down to crawl through the bushes to the cave's entrance, I braided my hair and fastened it at the end with a bobby pin. I'd had enough of catching it on twigs and kneeling on it when I crawled on my hands and knees.

It was a good feeling to go into the cave and know what I was doing this time. I felt quite brave and adventurous, since I didn't need to worry about what lay ahead. Even the slide through the tunnel seemed shorter than before.

This time, however, I was more cautious when I neared the bottom. I reached out on both sides and caught at the ropes so I wouldn't shoot clear out at the end of the tunnel. My blister opened and smarted, but I hung on and slowed myself so that when I reached the end I could stay just inside the tunnel mouth and look out into the bright afternoon sunlight of the glen.

It was a good thing I did. Once more, not all the men of the glen were goblins!

Below the grassy bank the little rock men were hurrying as usual, and now I knew some of them by name. King of the Hills stood up tall and commanding on my left—a big black rock with a spiked crown on its head. Clearly the king watched all that went on in the glen. Far on the other side scurried the Three Blind Mice, while The Marching Men marked time single file directly ahead. But over near the middle of the thickest goblin population, where Old Beak Nose should have stood among The Frightened Sisters—there was Galvin Sewell! His back was toward me and he was waving his arms in the most peculiar way. I could hear the strange whispery sounds he was making—sounds that chilled my blood because they carried such a menacing note.

It was my turn to spy on Galvin, instead of the other way around, and I stayed very still in the tunnel mouth, almost holding my breath. As I watched, he shook his finger and pointed. Then he gestured widely with a full sweep of both arms. All the leaning little goblins stood about him as quietly as though they listened to his odd whispering.

I couldn't make out the words, but after I had watched him for a few minutes I realized what he was doing. He was standing down there talking to the goblins. He was making them a speech with a great deal of angry feeling in it. This might have seemed a little crazy to me if I hadn't been up on a platform just a little while ago, making a speech to all Camberhills myself. Why shouldn't Galvin do the same thing if he felt like it?

I began to feel guilty about watching him. After all, Galvin had a right to daydream too, without anyone spying on him. I considered crawling out of the cave, turning around, and pulling myself back to the top. What I wanted was to have the glen to myself, and I couldn't do that with Galvin there. I might as well give up and not embarrass him with my sudden appearance.

But I was already too late. With a last wave of his arms he leaped upon one of the rocks and shouted out loud, so that the words went ringing and crackling around the glen. Now I heard them plainly enough.

"I'll show you!" he shouted. "You're not going to stop me— understand? Sooner or later you've got to tell the truth!"

Then he leaped from the rock, turned his back on all those secretive little men who knew what had happened long ago but weren't telling, and dashed up the bank, straight toward the tunnel—and me.

8 *A Flash of Light*

GALVIN saw me just as he reached the top of the bank.
He came to a halt and stood staring at me angrily. I crawled
out because there was nothing else to do, and stood up to
face him.

"You here again?" he said and scorn bit into the words.

I saw once more how tall and lanky he was—too thin for
his height—and how dark and angry his eyes always looked.
And I thought of how I had never seen him smile. I wished,
oddly enough, that I could make him cheer up and smile. I
wished he did not always need to be so angry with me.

"I only want to help!" I blurted out. "I'm not on Will
Horst's side the way you think."

"Help!" He snorted the word and his scorn only increased.
"You'd better watch it if you come down here alone. You're
no bigger than some of those goblins. What do you think will
happen to you if they catch you here alone?"

"You can't scare me like that," I snapped. "I'm not a baby,
even if I'm not very big."

He stared at me with those dark, intense eyes and I knew
he was willing me to be frightened. Willing me to go away.

"You mean you'll just laugh when they start to move around
down there?" he asked. "Laugh when they crowd in on you
and try to crush you with their weight as if you were no more
than a peanut."

I wouldn't let him frighten me. I wouldn't stand for it. Nobody could call me a peanut!

"What if I do what no one else has been able to do?" I cried. "What if I'm the one who is meant to find that money and give it back?"

He snorted again. "Then you'd better hurry up! Did you know my great-grandfather is dying? The doctor says he isn't going to live much longer. If he dies, he'll have to go knowing he has never paid off his debts, knowing all those people were ruined because of what happened to his bank. If you're a magician, you'd better act fast."

There was a sound like a sob in his voice and I knew what his anger hid. He swung away from me, dashed a quick hand across his eyes, and dived into the tunnel. The last I saw of him was the soles of his sneakers as he pulled himself upward into the rock slide.

All the angry feelings he had aroused in me faded out as I watched him go. I didn't want to be angry with Galvin Sewell. If he gave me a chance, I might even try to be his friend. But he was such a prickly boy there seemed to be no way to approach him. I felt sorry to hear about old Andrew Putney being ill. That seemed to make all my need to hurry come rushing back — and I could understand Galvin's desperate behavior all the better. He wasn't a juvenile delinquent as Tex had said. He was only a boy in a terrible hurry, a boy who had to fight a whole town because of what he believed.

The glen seemed empty and quiet around me with Galvin gone. The sun had slipped downward in the western sky, and I realized again that the deep heart of this place would be dark long before the rest of the countryside gave up its bright sunlight. Shadows were already long, but there was still time to look around by myself before the sun dropped out of sight behind the cliffs. And I wasn't really afraid in daylight, I told myself — no matter what Galvin had said.

I climbed down the bank and circled around The Marching Men — who looked determined enough to trample me down if I got in their way. Then I darted between them and The Witch's Sons. The Sons seemed to be wearing little peaked stone hats, with wicked little faces showing beneath, and they watched me with hollowed eyes as I ran past. But I couldn't avoid the main gathering of goblins, and as I walked slowly toward The Frightened Sisters, I wished Galvin hadn't put such horrid pictures into my mind. Especially since I could see, now that I was down here among them, that most of the goblin rocks were bigger than I was.

Nevertheless, I gritted my teeth, told myself not to be silly, and began to climb between the rocks and make my way toward the place I wanted most to see. At least The Frightened Sisters didn't look quite so much like goblin women close up as they did from a distance. I climbed among rough outcroppings of black rock that had streaks of mica shining through them, like the piece of rock Tex Myrick had given me from this very place.

There were spaces between the rock figures here and there, where earth had blown in and weedy grass had taken root. When I knelt in one of the center places and dug at the earth with a sharp stone, I found that the solid rock of the main base was underneath. This must surely be the place where Old Beak Nose was supposed to stand, but as others before me had already found, not one of the goblins nearby had anything that looked like a beak. They were all made of solid rock that joined the rock base underground. I tested this by trying to push at several of them to see if they would move, but everything was rooted solidly in granite. There was no likely place where a lot of money could have been hidden. The grassy earth covering patches in between was thin, with rock showing here and there near the surface, so there was not even a place to dig a real hole. Nothing about that map made any sense.

I sat down upon a round stone like a footstool, with tall black goblin women leaning above me, and wondered about the map. Why would everything in the glen be shown correctly —except for the one thing that marked where the treasure was hidden? Why would that be completely wrong?

A beaked nose would have to fit on a head. A head meant a rounded shape of some sort. There were a lot of rounded portions of rock that might be taken to look like heads. Some of them wore hats, some were bald, but not one of them had a beaked nose. There was even a loose, somewhat egg-shaped rock near where I sat that resembled a head. At some time in the distant past it must have been rolled over and over by torrents of water which had polished it almost smooth. But it had no protruding nose, and when I pushed it with an outstretched foot, it rolled over, unattached to anything. And it was certainly solid, not hollow. I looked around to see if it could have fallen from any of the rocks around me, but they were all solid too, with no loose parts. I got up and looked at the stone on which I was sitting and found that it was also unattached, but solid, with no holes in it.

As I stood there thinking about all this, something suddenly glinted in my eyes, almost blinding me with the flash. I put my head down to avoid the glare, and when I looked up again I saw nothing that could have caused a sudden flash like that. It must have come from the opposite side of the glen, across from where the sun was moving down toward the top of the cliffs, and I wondered if a car on a road up there had momentarily reflected sunlight into my eyes with its windshield or headlights.

I studied the far bank of cliffs more closely, and in a moment the light flashed in my eyes again — as though someone might be deliberately spotting me with a mirror. Quickly I moved away from the dazzle and got behind a tall rock goblin, where I could not be easily seen, and where I could peer around toward the tops of the cliffs. Yes — there was the shine of sun on glass again. Glass that moved and flashed as I watched — probably hunting for me. I knew what it was now. Someone up there was looking down into the glen with binoculars. Someone was watching every move I made. The knowledge made me thoroughly squirmy. All I wanted now was to get away, out of view of that mysterious watcher.

I had stayed as long as I wanted to, anyway, so I climbed out of the band of Frightened Sisters and started back for the tunnel. The watcher was behind me now and I couldn't tell if my movements were still being followed. I didn't turn around until I neared The Witch's Sons. Then I whirled abruptly and stared at the opposite cliffs. There was no flash of light, but I saw something I hadn't noticed before. The peaked roof of a

house stood up among the trees over there, and I could see squares of light shining in all its windows where the sun touched them. The glow from shining windows hadn't been visible down among the rocks, and it wasn't directed at me. The lower part of the house was lost among the trees, but it must be perched close to the edge of the cliffs. I wondered who lived there, and why the person was interested in spying on me.

The sudden barking of a dog caught my ear and I turned toward the tunnel in dismay. That had sounded like Chipper — and it was! The little dog was scampering up and down in front of the tunnel, and I had a sinking feeling that Tex and Florida would not be far behind him.

I was right. As I watched, Florida shot out first, and a moment later Tex came sledding down on a gunnysack pad. They both stood up, looking at me without surprise, and began to walk in my direction. Florida seemed different — perhaps because she had taken off her ruffly dress and put on jeans, and her blond hair looked blown and mussy. But her expression was different too. She stared at the ground as she walked beside her brother, instead of watching me in that bright malicious way of hers.

"Hi," Tex said, sounding as friendly as though I were an old pal by this time. "We saw the note you left, so we came down. Have you found anything?"

"You know I haven't," I said, watching him suspiciously, though he didn't seem to be making fun of me.

Florida raised her head and gave me a quick, hateful look. I knew she hadn't changed, even though her brother seemed to have tamed her for the moment.

"Florry hasn't told the Buddy Boys about the tunnel," Tex said. "And she isn't going to. I got hold of her in time. Maybe the three of us can start looking things over together. There's enough money to split three ways, if we find it."

"If we find it," I said, "it all goes to Andrew Putney. Did you know he's supposed to be dying? Galvin told me. He wants to find the answer more than ever, because his great-grandfather is so sick."

Tex and Florida exchanged a look and Florida stuck her chin out stubbornly. I suspected that she didn't care about Andrew Putney—she still wanted that money for her father. Which was silly, really, because he couldn't keep it. Florida seemed to make up her own rules inside her head and sometimes they didn't take into account what was real in the outside world. More than ever I was sure I wanted to do my hunting alone.

"We'd better go back," Tex said. "Mom's going to have supper early so she can get ready for company this evening. The Buddy Boys got hungry and went downtown to the diner without waiting for us."

"Buddy *Brothers*," Florida said impatiently and looked at me again. "You needn't have snitched on me. I wouldn't really have told anyone about the way down. I didn't mean what I said to Al Buddy."

"What if he thinks you meant it?" I asked. "What if he pins you down to keeping your promise?"

She tossed her blond head. "Then I'll think of something."

"It had better be good," Tex said. "Come on, let's go back."

Florida went up first and I followed, with Tex bringing Chipper and coming up last. It was easier for me this time. We reached the path that led toward the house and walked along talking about Galvin. I mentioned his name because I wanted to know why Tex had called him a juvenile delinquent.

Tex was willing enough to tell me. "Galvin's done a lot of things he shouldn't. He painted words on the meetinghouse fence: KEEP THE GLEN FOR CAMBERHILLS. They made him repaint the whole fence. Then there's the way he's been a nuisance to the men who are cutting a road into the glen. The second day after they started, some of their tools disappeared. Air has been let out of their car tires. And their caps and jackets have been carried off when they put them down. Whatever is taken always shows up someplace else, but it has made trouble and a lot of people are mad about it. Everyone knows that it's Galvin, but they haven't caught him at it, and warning him doesn't do any good. If other kids tease him, he gets into fights with them. It's pretty silly to think he can stop that road all by himself."

I could see that this was a foolish approach for Galvin, but somehow I felt increasingly sympathetic toward him. I kept feeling that he was in the right, more than Mr. Davidson or anyone else. He was just going about his fight in the wrong way. If he wasn't always so mad at me, perhaps I could make him understand that I was really on his side and wanted to find a way to help him.

When we reached the house I had time to get a bath, and afterward I put on a lemon-yellow dress with wide pleats and some gold-colored beads and patent leather slippers. Florida wasn't going to get ahead of me on being dressed up tonight. What's more, I got the tangles out of my hair and brushed it smooth. Its red color looked rather nice hanging over my shoulders against the yellow of my dress, I thought. And at least I wasn't fat like Florida. But I had to stand on tiptoe to see myself in the bureau mirror and I wondered for the thousandth time if I was ever going to grow.

Tonight we ate in the dining room, and when I came to the

table Mrs. Myrick said I looked very nice. Mr. Myrick gave
a welcoming smile, having left Athens in his typewriter, so
that he wasn't absentminded as he had been at lunch. Tex
hardly looked at me, being more interested in the meatballs
and spaghetti, which he was eating the way he did everything
else — slowly, as if he thought over every mouthful before he
swallowed it. Florida paid the most attention to me. She was
staring again, as though she wanted to find something to criti-
cize, and I was glad I'd taken some trouble with my appearance for once.

The Buddy Brothers had gone downtown to eat, Mrs. Myrick
said, because they wanted to have a look at the meetinghouse
where they would be performing, and Al wanted to check on
the car. The company coming tonight was to be in their honor,
so they had promised to return early.

"I've only invited a few people," Mrs. Myrick told us.
"Mr. Davidson asked if he could drop in to meet the boys and
bring his wife. And I've invited Rosalie Sewell too, and Galvin,
of course. After all, this is their house, and Rosalie is terribly
interested in everything connected with the festival."

"Why did you have to ask Galvin?" Tex muttered.

"Because I don't think we've been very nice to that boy,"
Mrs. Myrick said. "I can understand what he's going through
right now — with the glen being opened up, and his great-
grandfather ill. That boy is suffering. Rosalie says he feels the
whole town is against him, and I want to show him that we're
not."

"Good for us!" said Mr. Myrick, and I liked him all the better, because that was my feeling about Galvin too. I knew very
well that a person who was hurt could behave at his worst,
even when that was anything but sensible. Maybe I had a more
important project for my stay in Camberhills than the impos-
sible dream of finding that money. Perhaps my real project
was to make friends with Galvin Sewell and find a way to help
him. I had a quick memory of Dad saying, "When Trina gets
to be President, she'll fix up the world!" but I put it out of
my mind.

When their mother spoke about Galvin, Tex and Florida

looked at each other again, and I knew they didn't agree with her. It might be a good idea tonight if I kept an eye on both of them—just in case they thought of some new way to torment Galvin. There might be a chance for me to talk to him tonight. Anyway, I meant to try.

Somewhere in the back of my mind an idea was stirring. It was only a hint of an idea, really—a kind of maddening glimmer that slipped away when I tried to look at it closely. It had something to do with that stone which hadn't seemed to belong with anything else. Where had it come from? How had it got there? And did that matter, anyway? Perhaps Galvin would know. But I needed to pin down my feeling about it more clearly first. I had to find out why it bothered me.

9 *Disaster in the Evening*

AL AND JOE kept their promise and by the time the dishes were done, they were back at the house. We all sat in slatted wooden chairs out on the big veranda. It was lovely there, with the dusk gathering, pulling everything in close and snug around us. The woods were all around the house, but the wide stretch of grass held the trees away, so they couldn't come too near with their black circle of shadows.

After the hot day, the evening was pleasantly cool, and there was a good feeling about sitting there together, not doing anything special. My mother would have loved this and I had a wistful feeling about missing her. It was very peaceful, very quiet. I didn't know it then, but I suppose this was the calm before the storm that lay ahead. At least for me.

Al sat apart from the rest of us, rocking in an old-fashioned wicker chair, lost in his own thoughts, and perhaps a little bored. Joe had folded his long self onto the top veranda step and was watching the fireflies that flickered in and out near the lilac bushes and over against the woods. I had never seen so many fireflies in my life.

Joe Buddy was really interested in those fireflies. After a while he went down the steps to catch one, and when he brought it back he showed me how it flicked its tiny bulb on and off, glowing green-gold in his cupped hand. Then he tossed it back to freedom and it went fluttering off to join its kinfolk dancing against the dark woods.

Al watched his brother as he came back to the veranda,

and suddenly he sat straight up in his rocker.

"Hey," he said, "have you been cutting your hair?"

Joe kept right on watching the fireflies, not looking at Al. "Not enough to spoil the act," he said, though it was clear that his hair was shorter than his brother's.

There was an uncomfortable silence and I think we all sensed the bristling that went on between the Buddy Brothers.

"Styles change and the young like to be different from their elders," Mrs. Myrick said cheerfully. "That is, until you become elders too and it's your turn to disapprove of what your young people are doing and wearing. Wait—I've just thought of a jangle! I've got it—I think—all but the last line. Listen to this:

> "The sheik of Araby
>> Has vanished with the past;
>> His grandsons sport a new hairdo—"

She looked expectantly at her husband, who supplied a last line promptly: "—But neither will it last."

Al Buddy creaked his rocker around and looked down the veranda. "What's all this?" he asked. "What's a jangle?"

Mrs. Myrick explained that jangles were a family invention of their own, and started another one.

> "Crew cut, crew cut,
>> Whither have you gone?
>> Long locks, long locks,
>> Will you last till dawn?"

Al Buddy chortled. "You're not talking about my hair, are you?"

"Try one yourself," Mr. Myrick said. "Like this—

> "Times change and customs too;
>> So did I and so will you."

Al thought for a few minutes. "All right," he said, "how's this for a start?

> "You are old and therefore wrong,
>> I am young and bold and strong.

I am young and know so much,
You are old and out of touch!"

Florida clapped her hands furiously in applause and both
Mr. and Mrs. Myrick laughed. Tex made a grunting sound, as
though he didn't mean to agree with anything Al Buddy said,
and threw his sister a disgusted look.

Joe did not join in either the applause or the laughter. He
went quietly along the veranda to his room, and was back in a
moment bringing his big wooden guitar with him.

His brother saw him at once. "Looks as if we've got a show-
off here," he said, but Joe paid no attention.

With those dark glasses gone, Joe's face seemed less secretive, less gloomy. I had a feeling that he liked the country and
the summer night, and he didn't let what his brother said disturb him as he sat down once more on the veranda steps. He
held the big wooden guitar almost lovingly and began to plunk
a few notes, tuning the strings. I doubted his words about not
caring if it was smashed to bits.

Florida perched on the arm of a chair not far from me, and I
saw her little wriggle of anticipation over what was to come.
Mr. Myrick didn't exactly groan, because he was being polite,
but I had a feeling that he would not enjoy the sort of music
that was coming. What the Buddy Brothers did was sometimes
folk-rock and it had a pretty strong beat, the way we like it
today.

Mrs. Myrick nodded her approval. "How lovely! You're
going to sing for us, Joe. Aren't you going to join in, Al?"

"Without a mike?" Al said and I heard a bite in his voice
as though something did not please him. "No — this isn't my
speed. My brother's a bit of a square, I'm afraid. You'll have
to bear with him."

Joe neither smiled nor scowled. It was almost as if he were
doing this for himself and didn't care much whether anyone
else listened or not. When he began to sing I stared at him in
surprise. This wasn't what you'd expect of a Buddy Brother.
This was an old song — "Harbor Lights" — and he sang it softly,
true and on key. Somehow the music and the words and the

summer night made me choke up in an unexpected way. Joe's voice sounded unbearably, beautifully, sad. After that he sang "They Call the Wind Maria" and "Tumbleweed" and "In a Little Spanish Town." He seemed to like songs of the Southwest and sea songs. Pretty soon we were making requests of our own, and Joe Buddy was picking them all up. He seemed to know the words and tune to almost anything—but nothing he sang was the sort of thing the boys were famous for.

I found myself wondering about him more and more. In some ways he was like an older Galvin—gloomy and distrustful. But not now, while he was singing all those old-fashioned songs. In a way, I suppose I was disappointed, and I knew Florida was too—because it would have been exciting to have a private, just-for-us show by the Buddy Brothers. But Joe looked so relaxed and peaceful that I couldn't hold it against him for disappointing us.

Al was the only one who didn't like the songs at all. He sat by himself in his rocker halfway down the veranda from the rest of us, looking plain bored. Sometimes he moved his chair so that it creaked in protest. When they were on mike, the show was mainly his, and while his voice wasn't as good as Joe's, it fitted songs like "How Do I Get Along?" which was their latest pop record. Everybody said it would give them another goldie.

The music didn't stop until Mr. Davidson and his wife drove up, bringing Rosalie Sewell and Galvin with them. They came up on the veranda and were all introduced to the Buddy Brothers. Then the senior selectman and his wife were introduced to me. He was a tall, rather good-looking man, very lively and enthusiastic. I could tell right away that he was terribly eager for the festival to be a success, and sincere about what he hoped his entire plan would do for the town. By profession he was a lawyer in Camberhills, since his selectman's post wasn't a full-time job. He made a very big thing out of welcoming Al and Joe to the town, as if he were bestowing the Keys of the City upon them, the way they do in bigger places.

Mrs. Davidson was a quiet little woman with eyes that

sparkled their approval of her husband. She and Mrs. Myrick were already friends, and of course Rosalie Sewell knew them both. Apparently Mr. Davidson was a fan when it came to Hugh Myrick's books, and he settled down to ask a few questions about Mr. Myrick's last spy story.

I was more interested in Galvin than in the others. He was the one who made me most curious. I noticed that he kept a long way off from Tex and Florida, and I was sure he wasn't here tonight because he wanted to be. But at least he was human enough to be curious about Al and Joe Buddy because he kept watching them in a wondering way, as if they were creatures who had just landed from another planet. Somehow I couldn't imagine Galvin letting his hair grow long.

When everyone had been introduced, Mrs. Myrick and Florida went inside to bring lemonade and cookies. I offered to help, but Mrs. Myrick said to stay and get acquainted. So I moved my chair along the veranda until I was opposite the place where Galvin had draped his lanky self against the rail. He was paying absolutely no attention to me, and I could see there wouldn't be much opportunity to say anything to him. I meant to watch for my chance, just in case. I wished I could toss out some surprising, tantalizing remark that would get him to see me as a person. No matter how many times he stepped on my toes, I always had the feeling that he was somehow a boy in disguise, and that he would be someone else if I could get past his guard. Of course I couldn't guess then about the awful thing he would do to me before the evening was over. That still lay ahead.

While I couldn't think of anything really attention-getting to say to him, I managed to put one question under cover of the others' talk.

"Who owns that house that's built on the rim of the cliffs?" I asked. "The house on the eastern side, above the glen?"

Galvin stared at Al Buddy and took so long to answer that I thought he might not have heard me. Then he turned his usual annoyed look in my direction as though I was a terrible nuisance and he couldn't bear the sight of me.

"That's our house," he said. "That's where we live, since

we can't live here." He put so much resentment into the words that I knew he must feel this was his rightful home, and that we had no business in it. Now I began to see an answer to what had happened this afternoon.

"Then it was you watching me through glasses when I was down in the glen," I said. "You went home after you left me and—"

"I did not!" he said indignantly. "I went straight downtown. What are you talking about?"

I had a feeling that he was telling the truth, and if that was so, I was no farther ahead than before. If it wasn't Galvin who watched me, this was still another puzzle I must look into.

Mrs. Myrick and Florida came back with trays, and we sat around drinking cold lemonade and eating cookies. After a while Mr. Davidson began to talk to the Buddy Brothers, asking Al how he and Joe felt about being so successful. And what about their educations? Had they finished college?

Al was pleasant enough, but a little superior, I thought, as though a small-town selectman wasn't very important to him.

"A year of college was enough for me," he said. "We were working our way at the same time, and it was too rough to keep it up. We couldn't accept engagements, and there wasn't much point to studying when we could make so much money this way. It looks as if we can go on for a few years and make enough to keep us in the future, no matter what happens."

Ever since the company had arrived, Joe had been sitting silently in his place on the steps, with his guitar quiet across his knees. Now he looked at Mr. Davidson, and then at his brother.

"One more year, anyway," he said. "Then that's it. I'm going back to finish school."

"Joe has rocks in his head." Al sounded scornful and impatient, as though this was an old argument.

Now I understood at least one reason for the quarrel that seemed to run between the two brothers. Al liked what he was doing, and Joe didn't. Joe wanted to get back to school, but Al needed him if he was to keep on being one of the popular Buddy Brothers.

Miss Sewell leaned forward in her chair in her bright, interested way and spoke to Joe. "What will you do when you graduate? Will you go back to this sort of thing?"

"Not if I can help it," Joe said, and tightened his lips over the words.

Mr. Davidson must have sensed deep waters here, because he turned to Mrs. Myrick, changing the subject.

"I hope you don't mind," he said, "but I've asked Bill Eckers of the *Camberhills Crier* to drop over this evening to get an interview with the Buddy Brothers. This is the county paper, you know, and we'd like a front-page write-up about our distinguished guests as publicity for the festival. You don't mind, do you, boys?"

Mrs. Myrick murmured that it was all right with her, and Al Buddy said, "Sure, fine," cheerfully enough. Joe said nothing, and Galvin, who had been so quiet at his place by the rail that I think everyone had forgotten about him, made the sort of growling sound I'd heard before when he was angry about something.

Mr. Davidson heard him too, and looked slightly irritated. Galvin must have been a thorn in the side of the town's pet project for some time, and now he pinned Galvin down deliberately.

"Perhaps it will be interesting for Bill to find out how you and Rosalie and your great-grandfather feel about the festival," Mr. Davidson said. "And about how you feel concerning our coming plans for Camberhills."

This was a direct challenge, but Miss Sewell answered quickly, before her brother could growl again. "Of course we'll help in any way we can. We owe the town a great deal for its kindness to us over the years. Galvin doesn't feel exactly as I do, but perhaps the story will be all the more interesting if Bill Eckers covers his viewpoint too."

Mr. Myrick chuckled softly and I knew he was pleased with her words, and the way she had, in a sense, put Mr. Davidson in a corner where he had to let Galvin have his say. Maybe if Galvin could express himself right out where everyone could read his words and understand how he felt, he might feel better about everything. If only Galvin would realize this and not get mad, it was a real opportunity for him.

But Galvin was already mad. "Now I suppose that bank holdup story will come out in the papers all over again!" he said. "Why doesn't anybody think about how my great-grandfather feels? The way Mr. Eckers writes sometimes, he'll probably make it sound funny, and — "

Mr. Davidson was shaking his head, unwilling to let Galvin finish. "Don't get yourself so easily upset, boy. Forty years can turn something into interesting history. This is a colorful story. Not a town around here has such a story to tell about as interesting a place as our own Goblin Glen. The more romantic the story sounds, the more people it will bring to Camberhills."

I looked at Mr. Myrick to see how he was reacting to this, and I was glad when he leaned forward and broke into what Mr. Davidson was saying.

"Don't you think there may be a danger in letting past evil-doing come to seem romantic?" he asked.

The selectman looked surprised and Mr. Myrick went on. "Billy the Kid was a murderer. So was Adolf Hitler. Do we want to let time make us forget these things?"

Mr. Davidson wouldn't accept Mr. Myrick's words as applying here, and he went off into another long stream of words.

I stopped listening. I probably came closer to understanding how Galvin felt than anyone else here, except his sister, and I was glad Mr. Davidson didn't know about my own relationship to the Horsts or he might have tried to get some horrible publicity out of that too. I could imagine how awful it would be if the town knew—with everyone staring at me when I went along Main Street, and thinking there must be bad blood in my family. Or even thinking that my father ought to pay up for something a distant in-law had done long ago. Will Horst wasn't my fault, but by this time I didn't enjoy being related to him. It was bad enough having Galvin and Miss Sewell and the Myricks know about this.

At last Mr. Davidson paused for breath and Galvin spoke up again, so I began to listen, without the slightest preparation for what he was about to do to me.

"If you really want a good story," Galvin said, "maybe Mr. Eckers had better interview Trina Corey too. Did you know that Will Horst is her great-uncle? I'll bet a lot of people will be interested to know there's a Horst back in town."

It was as though I had been standing near the edge of a road feeling perfectly safe, with no traffic coming—when suddenly a car jumped out of empty space to knock me down. I could hardly get my breath. I felt so stunned. Later I remembered sounds around me: Miss Sewell's gasp, Al Buddy's rocking chair creak, Mrs. Myrick's little cry of dismay—but I couldn't sort them out just then. I couldn't look at anyone. I put my head down so my hair fell across my face in a red curtain.

Mr. Davidson bounced with excitement. Even though I wasn't looking, I could tell that by his voice. "How wonderful!" he cried. "This means we've got a much bigger story here than I ever guessed. Why—this is a story the big state papers will pick up and reprint. We couldn't wish for better publicity.

Wait till I talk to Bill Eckers!"

This was awful. It was getting worse every minute and there was no place for me to hide except behind my hair.

It was Mr. Myrick who answered him quite evenly and calmly. "If your Bill Eckers puts anything about Trina in his story, I will personally knock his block off," he said, smiling gently—and meaning every word, just like one of his own spy heroes.

I could have hugged him, but I knew I was going to cry in a minute, and I couldn't bear to have them all see. I jumped up and ran for the door to the house. Somehow Joe Buddy was there ahead of me, opening the screen.

"Take it easy," he said as I dashed inside.

I almost banged into the marble Venus at the foot of the stairs, because tears were blinding me, but I managed to duck her and run up the steps as fast as I could go. I tore down the upper hall to my room and rushed inside, banging the door behind me. Then I dived for the middle of my bed and lay there in the dark with my nose buried in the pillow, not trying to choke off my sobs. All I wanted right then was to be safely home with my mother and father, and far away from this awful place where people could be so cruel. Galvin was the most awful boy I had ever known, and I hated him with all my heart.

10 *Serenade*

ALMOST at once the door I had banged opened softly, and someone came into the room. She pulled up a chair and sat down close to the bed, not touching me, just speaking to me gently.

"Mrs. Myrick wanted to come," Rosalie Sewell said, "but I asked her to let me, since this is my brother's fault. I can't tell you how sorry I am. I don't know what gets into Galvin lately. Because he's angry and hurt, he wants to hurt everyone else."

Now I really cried, feeling terribly sorry for myself. My pillowcase was quickly wet and I could hardly breathe for long, choking sobs. In a muddled sort of way I remembered Mr. Myrick bringing me to Camberhills from the airport, and stopping to show me Goblin Glen so I would understand that the story of Will Horst wasn't a distant romance, but something that had happened to real people. No one needed to tell me how real it was now. It was still happening — and happening to me!

Miss Sewell let me cry for a little while, and then she took hold of my elbow to give it a little shake. "Time to snap out of it," she said. She reached out and pushed my hair back from my face. "Sit up and let's try this in a couple of side ponytails," she said. "It's a very perky style and you'll be a lot more comfortable."

I almost sobbed again. How could she talk about *hair* when this awful thing had happened to me? Nevertheless, I let her pull me up from the bed and get my comb and brush. It was soothing to let her brush my hair—and not think about anything for a while. She brushed in long strokes and electricity crackled.

By the time Mrs. Myrick came upstairs to bring me a glass of milk, I felt better and not so much alone. She set the glass on a table and nodded in approval over my hair.

"Mr. Eckers is here," she told Miss Sewell. "He'd like to talk to you, if you don't mind."

"What about Galvin?" Miss Sewell asked quickly.

Mrs. Myrick looked upset. "Your brother went off by himself right after you came upstairs. I expect he knew how unpopular he was going to be."

"Will Mr. Davidson tell—" I began, and Mrs. Myrick shook her head.

"No, he won't say a word. He wanted a good story in the paper, but he was thoughtless about how you might feel. He was sorry right away, so you needn't worry. Mr. Eckers is talking to the Buddy Brothers and Al is giving him a big story about how he would like to dig up that long-lost money. There will be plenty to write about. Of course Al isn't going to find anything, any more than anyone else is likely to, but this will add publicity interest to Mr. Davidson's plan for bringing in visitors. No one needs to mention you, Trina dear."

Miss Sewell stood up. "I'll go downstairs right away. Don't worry, Trina. I'm going to give Galvin a real talking to. I don't think your relationship to the Horsts matters, but if you feel sensitive about it, then we must respect your feelings."

Mrs. Myrick had to return to her guests, so I sat in a chair, sipping milk and staring at the bust of Petrarch on his pedestal behind the door. It didn't bother me anymore to have him around. Somehow he was beginning to seem like a proper part of the room. From where I sat I could only see his profile—a proud, aristocratic profile, with a long, beaked nose. The nose caught my attention because it reminded me of something I had seen somewhere.

I finished the last swallow of milk and jumped up to view Mr. Petrarch more closely. His marble nose was slightly chipped at the end, but the curve was strong and hooked, as a bird's beak is hooked. That was it, of course. That was what caught my attention and made me think of Old Beak Nose, who was mentioned on the map in the library.

Or was it that? I had the oddest feeling that I had seen a nose just like this somewhere else. Not only on Mr. Petrarch, but somewhere, somewhere . . .

I couldn't remember where. Not in the glen, surely. I had done nothing but look for beaked noses when I was down among the goblins.

From outside came the sound of car doors slamming, motors starting, the sound of good-bys as the company drove away. So the editor of the *Crier* had his story and was going off to write it—luckily without Trina Corey having any part in it. And no thanks to Galvin Sewell. I was through trying to take his side. Through for good. If I could find a way, I would be as mean to him as he had been to me.

Tears were ready to come again, and I had to blink hard to hold them back. I had never offered him anything but friend-ship, and in return he had been mean, mean, mean.

From outside in the night came another sound—as though someone had struck a chord on a guitar just under my window. I stood up, startled, listening—and heard voices begin to sing. What I heard was hard to believe. It couldn't really be happen-ing. That was the Buddy Brothers' hit tune and Al and Joe were singing out there—singing right under my window!

I ran over to look—and there they were. A big full moon had risen over the pine trees and the lawn was bright silver. Full in the glow of light stood Al and Joe—exactly the way I had seen them so many times on television, except that this time Joe held his wooden guitar and Al's hands were empty. Electric guitars wouldn't do much good out here. Both boys were looking right up at me as they sang words I certainly knew by heart.

> "How do I get along without you?
> How do I get along?
> How do I get along without you?
> How do I ever, ever get along?"

I could remember Dad saying the Buddy songs were on the
monotonous side, but I didn't care. This was being sung
for me!

All I could do was look down at them, hardly believing this
was happening to me. I didn't even hear Florida Myrick when
she came into the room. I didn't know she was there until she
stood beside me. The boys saw her and Al gave her a little
bow. After that, they included her in their serenade, and it was
all so wonderful that I didn't mind sharing. I was so happy that
I wanted everyone else to be happy too. I even slipped my
hand through the crook of Florida's arm, and she didn't
pull away, but gave me a quick sidelong smile.

This was something I would surely remember all my life,
I thought. I wanted the moment never to end. Maybe more
important things than this would happen to me—but hardly
anything could have more feeling in it. I didn't need to daydream—a daydream was happening to me right now.

Of course it did end. The boys came to their usual flourish

and stopped. They both bent from the waist with their heads down, making the sort of bow they always made to the thousands who watched them. Only this time there was just Florida and me to watch. We both clapped until our palms stung, and maybe we added a few squeals for the fun of it.

The boys made another bow, and then Al shook his long hair back from his eyes and came close beneath the window. "Hey, you two Juliets," he called up to us, "how about giving us the secret of how to get down to the glen?"

I wished he hadn't said that. Somehow it spoiled what had gone before. When I remembered tonight, I would have to cut this part off in my mind. Beside me, Florida was still in a trance, and she was already opening her mouth to answer. I tightened my hand on her arm and she gave me a quick look and gulped. Then she looked down at Al.

"Sure — I'll tell you," she said, and pulled away as I pinched her. For a minute I thought all was lost. Then she went on. "If you want to do some climbing, I suppose you can get down through the rocks in the cut. But it's very dangerous that way. Don't try it at night."

Al looked up at her doubtfully and Joe laughed.

"Ask a silly question, get a silly answer," Joe said. "Anybody who tries to get through that cut has more rocks in his head than I have. I looked at it this afternoon. You'd break your neck. The cut is out."

Al wouldn't give up. He smiled teasingly at Florida. "Oh, come on. There's a better way. We all know that. How about telling us, baby?"

I was afraid of what that smile would do to Florida, and I spoke before she could answer him. "Why do you want to know? What good would it do you?"

Al's smile flashed again, all the more appealing in the moonlight. "Oh, I don't know — maybe I feel lucky. And maybe we're going to need a lot of money if my little brother here goes back to school and leaves me stranded."

Because of Florida, I didn't dare talk to him any longer. I could practically feel her weakening. I stepped quickly back from the window and pulled her with me. I'm not sure why I had such a strong feeling against telling Al Buddy about the secret tunnel down the cliff. Surely it wasn't all that important. What could he find — any more than anyone else?

Florida jerked away from me and I knew she was ready to go back to the window.

"Remember what Tex said," I warned her. Then I went to the wall and edged along it until I could look down from behind the curtains without being seen. Both boys were walking around the house out of sight.

"They're gone," I said. "It's safe now."

She stood staring at me across the room as if I had injured her in some way. "He'll hate me," she said. "And it will be your fault. Everything is getting to be your fault." She meant Al, of course, not Joe. She always meant Al.

This was so unfair that I could feel myself getting angry again, and I tried to hang onto my temper. It seemed such a waste of time to go on fighting with Florida Myrick when I had to spend the summer in her house. Since she wouldn't try to make friends with me, maybe it was up to me to do the trying. After all, I still felt pretty good over what had just happened. There would be no ugly story in the paper, and I — we — had just been serenaded by the Buddy Brothers. I couldn't feel as gloomy as Florida looked. So I swallowed my irritation and smiled at her as cheerfully as I could.

"You know something?" I said. "I'll bet we're the only two girls in the whole world who have been sung to all by ourselves by Al and Joe Buddy."

It was remarkable how unpretty a pretty girl could look when she made the sort of face Florida was making — pouting and cross and resentful.

"*You* were sung to — not me," she said.

I stared at her in astonishment. "Don't be silly. It only started out being for me — because my feelings had been hurt and they wanted to cheer me up. It ended up for both of us. For you as much as me."

Florida shook her head and the fluffy blond hair I envied danced on either side of her face. "Nobody would ever sing to me. I'm too fat. I'm fat and horrible, and boys snicker behind my back at school, and—and—" She broke off and for a minute I had a dreadful feeling that she was going to burst into tears.

I suppose I stared at her with my mouth open because I couldn't think of anything to say. I was too surprised. Here I had thought she was conceited and too pleased with herself, when all the while she was worried about being fat.

"Why are you making such a face?" she demanded, choking back her tears and frowning at me. "You look like a goldfish with your mouth open like that."

I felt like saying, "Who's making a face?" but I didn't, because all of a sudden I'd had a glimpse of what Florida Myrick felt like inside and I wondered if it was that way with everyone. Maybe I wasn't the only one who put up a bluff and over-acted because I thought I had something to overcome. The thought made me feel a bit kinder toward Florida, in spite of the way she behaved.

"I'm just surprised," I told her. "You're not all that fat. And besides, fat is something you can lose if you want to enough. I've been thinking how lucky you are to be pretty and have lovely hair and not be a half-pint like me."

She blinked once or twice, and then started for the door. I thought she was going to walk straight out without another word, but once more she surprised me. She stopped before she went into the hall and spoke without looking back.

"If you want to come to my room for a while, I've got some Buddy records. Maybe we could play them. If you want to."

Then she walked out without waiting for an answer. I felt something like a bursting of relief inside me. Even though I could be scrappy when I got mad, I really didn't like fight-ing with people. I went right after Florida and followed her into her room, ready to be friends if she'd let me.

Her room was interesting and not like any I'd ever seen. It was exactly right for this old house. Apparently Florida liked to draw and paint, because the torn, faded wallpaper on one wall had been almost hidden with large pictures she had made and tacked up over its surface. She was especially good at drawing people—where I could only draw them from the back because I could never make faces look like faces. Florida had done a drawing of Tex with his rock collection, another one of Mr. Myrick sitting at his desk, with a whole dreamworld of spy characters floating out of his typewriter. There was a lovely one of Mrs. Myrick too, apparently lecturing to an audience of marble busts. And my friend Petrarch was there, nose and all. It was surprising to find that Florida had a sense of humor. With all the meanness I'd seen, I had never expected this.

"If I could draw as well as you can," I told her, "I wouldn't mind being so small."

She gave me what almost passed for a smile and led the way to a tower alcove that opened off a corner of her room. Here padded window seats circled a low table with a record player on it. I didn't need to ask whose records were stacked in a deck, ready to go.

She turned on the machine and a record dropped into place, the arm swished over, and the needle found its groove. Florida ran to a lamp switch and turned off the light. At once moonlight flooded through the circling windows of the tower and both of us curled up on window seats, me with my knees pulled up under my chin, Florida leaning back against a pile of cushions, as we listened to the voice coming out of the darkness. That was Al Buddy, with both electric guitars in the background, and then Joe's voice joining in on the first chorus, but kept as an accompaniment, and not the way it could be when he sang alone as he had on the veranda this evening. The beat was there—the Big Beat that made their music really hit us, and I found myself rocking to it on the window seat, keeping time.

Of course listening to these records tonight was something special. Special because the real Al and Joe were under this very roof. Perhaps they could hear the echo of their own voices drifting out into the night, and know we were still listening to them.

Florida had her eyes closed and she had stopped looking sullen and cross, so I knew the beat of the music had reached her. The words didn't matter so much—though that was some-

thing grown-ups never seemed to understand. "What *is* all
that yeah-yeah stuff?" Dad is always asking me. But how do
you explain a sort of blurry, joyful feeling that fades out all
your troubles while you listen to it, and move to it? Dad, being
an editor, always thinks everything can be turned into words,
and he tries to get me to explain. How do you describe a
thumping inside that keeps time to some special beat of music
and gives you a feeling that life is wonderful and exciting — with
all sorts of lovely things lying ahead that are sure to happen?
Afterward, when the music stops, you feel better and your
worries about school, or that argument you had with your
parents, or your wanting to do something you know you can't
do — all these things that knot you up inside let go, dissolve,
fade out, so that afterward you can give your attention to
things you really do know are more important — and do them
better. Once when I tried to explain this to Dad, he said,
"Hah — catharsis!" — whatever he meant by that.

But there — I'm trying to put it into words now, and it
doesn't work. "Mindless," Dad calls it. Maybe that's the
point — just to stop once in a while and *feel* with all of yourself. I've seen my mother stand on a crosstown street in New
York and look down some concrete canyon, west toward
where the sun is setting across the Hudson — and I know she
isn't thinking, Blue, gold, pink — she's just feeling.

Only — and here was the strange thing — tonight I wasn't
feeling the music as much as usual. I was thinking instead. The
voices I knew so well, the over-and-over-again beat was there,
but I wasn't jumping to it. I wasn't lost in a dream the way
Florida was. My mind was all wound up and busier than ever
because I kept remembering all kinds of strange things.

For instance, I remembered how interested Al was in the
legend of the lost money. As if he might find it and keep it for
himself — which of course wasn't possible. I was thinking too
of Joe's quiet ways, his gloomy expression, and how he could
be unexpectedly kind, as he was when he hurried to open the
screen door for me tonight when I ran into the house. Of
course I thought about Galvin too and of how despicable he
had been. And of how nice Rosalie Sewell was. She made me

feel that I didn't need to worry about being related to Will Horst. I even thought of Florida Myrick and the surprise she had handed me this evening.

The record came to an abrupt end, the machine made a whispering sound, and there was a click as the next record dropped into place.

Suddenly I spoke above the thrumming of the Buddy guitars. "Florida, why did you tell Al he could get down to the glen by way of the cut?"

She came out of her trance and looked at me blankly for a moment. "Because he can't. Even if he tried, he wouldn't do it at night, and in the daytime the men working on the road would stop him. But I wish I could have told him the truth about the tunnel. Then maybe he'd like me, even if I am fat."

"You promised Tex," I reminded her sternly. "But why should he have such a strong notion about going down to the glen anyway?"

Florida shrugged, apparently finding nothing strange about Al's determination.

Just then there was a tap on the door and it opened to let light from the hall paint a long path across the floor. We looked around, blinking, and Mrs. Myrick smiled at us from the doorway.

"It has been a lovely evening, after all, hasn't it?" she said. "I heard the boys singing to you. But lovely evenings have to end, and I'm afraid it's past bedtime, girls."

Reluctantly Florida reached out to stop the record player, and Al's voice ended on a dragged-out note. I got up and stretched widely, discovering how sleepy I was. I knew I would sleep soundly now. I wasn't so upset anymore.

I had no idea then of what was coming tomorrow.

11 *Mr. Petrarch's Nose*

I MUST have been asleep for quite a long time. The darkness of the room had that middle-of-the-night feeling when I wakened suddenly from my dreaming. Dreams slip away quickly if you let them go, but I've found that if I lie quietly, remembering them right away, a lot of what I dreamed comes back.

There was something about this dream which seemed so important that I lay trying to hold on to it, wishing I could push it a little farther along so that an answer I was searching for could be given me.

In the dream Petrarch had started to talk to me from his corner, instead of listening, as he usually did. "I would like to tell you about my nose," he said. "It's very important for you to understand about my nose."

There had been more to that weird conversation and there had been some very queer action in the dream, because the marble Mr. Petrarch and I didn't stay put in my room. I don't know what he was walking on, since he had no legs, but we seemed to be out of my room and drifting through the woods. At least he drifted, with me running to keep up with him. He seemed to be wearing some sort of long white Roman toga that hung to the ground and concealed his means of movement. I remember thinking that he was following his long nose right through the woods toward the place where the tunnel cut down through the cliff.

But before we got to wherever he was taking me, and before

he finished discussing the importance of his nose, something wakened me. This much I could remember, but no more. It seemed as though he had made some special remark about his nose that had brought me a feeling of excited recognition. I had felt quite triumphant about it in my dream.

Now I was half awake, and no matter how I tried, the details were already slipping drowsily away. In a minute I would fall asleep again. Outdoors a strong wind had blown up in the night and I could hear it sighing and whispering in the tops of the pine trees. Through the wind sound something else penetrated. Another sound—perhaps the sound that had wakened me.

I flung off my covers and sat up in bed. The moon had gone around to the other side of the sky and the night wasn't as bright as it had been earlier. A pleasantly cool breeze blew in and touched my face as I slipped out of bed and went barefoot to the side window to look out into the night. The lawn that ran to the edge of the woods seemed gray instead of green, and it was empty of anything that moved. Bushes and a tree or two made dark, stationary shadows, but I could see no human forms down there on the grass. Yet I had a feeling that it was soft voices that had wakened me.

Since mine was an end room, and closer to the woods than any other, I would be the one to hear if someone was talking down there. Voices didn't drift around by themselves and—there!—I'd heard it again! This time I had a direction. Whoever whispered did it within the shelter of the woods themselves, and that probably meant at the entrance to the path.

I knelt at the windowsill, the better to see out across the lawn. Somewhere behind the trees a light came on, moved, vanished. Someone down there was using a flashlight. I could feel my heart thumping now because this was really exciting. Whoever it was had chosen an hour when everyone else should be asleep, and that meant movements that were secret and mysterious.

As I watched, the flashlight beam streaked across the lawn, someone whispered warningly in a low voice, and the light disappeared. Two figures emerged from the woods. They wore dark jackets and trousers, so they became hardly more than shadows themselves, though it wasn't hard for me to tell who they were. I sank even lower on the floor, so that just my eyes peered over the sill. I didn't want the Buddy Brothers to look up at my window and catch me watching them in the night.

Suddenly one figure crouched low and made a dash across the grayish space of the lawn. A moment later Al followed his brother, swaggering across slowly, as though he didn't care who might see him. Both of them disappeared around the end of the house. Now I could kneel and look out at the empty night without being seen.

Why on earth had Al and Joe Buddy been searching the woods so secretly at this late hour? If they thought the only way into the glen was through the cut, as Florida had said, surely they would have gone over there—far away from the house. But of course this meant they didn't believe her. Somehow they knew there was another way down and they must have been out looking for it while everyone else was asleep. I was sure they hadn't found it. I wouldn't have found it myself, even by daylight, if Chipper hadn't shown me the way.

Somehow what I had just seen left me uneasy. There seemed to be something unpleasantly secret about all this. Al had boasted openly about how he meant to hunt for the lost money himself. Then why was he moving secretly through the woods at night? And where did Joe stand in all this?

I didn't know, and my knees hurt from kneeling on the bare floor. I stood up and rubbed them, looking vaguely around my room at the same time, as if for an answer. Mr. Petrarch made a white blob in the darkness and I knew he watched me with his empty marble eyes. Suddenly I knew what he had said to me in my dream.

"My nose is like a rock," he'd said. "My nose is like a curved beak of a rock."

I went to where he stood by the door, and he didn't frighten me anymore. I ran my fingers over his nose and found that it really was a curved rock of a nose. So what? Why had that seemed so important to me in my dream that I could still feel— ever so faintly—the triumphant thrill that had gone through me?

A rock? Where had I seen a rock like Petrarch's nose?

Hoping no one would notice or come to ask what was wrong, I turned on my light and went to the tall old-fashioned bureau with the mirror over it. My chin didn't come quite to the top, but my eyes could search its surface readily enough. And there, waiting for me, was the meaning of the dream.

I reached for the black rock Tex Myrick had given me to help start my collection, and carried it over to a lamp to examine it more closely. The shape of it was very much like Petrarch's nose, as well as like the beak of a bird. Only the rock was larger. A large, strong rock nose that Tex had picked up somewhere down in the glen!

It wasn't much to go on, of course. There must be hundreds of rocks down there that looked like this one. Still, it really did resemble a nose. Under the beaked curve there were two faint indentations that were almost like nostrils. If such a stone were stuck onto a rock face, it would look like a nose, all right. Enough so that someone might have used the term "Old Beak Nose" to describe any face it belonged to.

Only it *wasn't* part of any face. All those goblins down there were made of solid rock. So sound and solid that they certainly weren't losing their noses, if they had any. I turned the heavy thing over in my hands, watching the shine of mica catch the light in the grainy black surface. What might the rest of the face be like? Hollow-eyed, perhaps, with ugly fangs at the mouth? Or would the nose belong to a smooth, egg-shaped stone head? One like the rock I had seen lying loose among The Frightened Sisters? Down there in that very place which Will Horst had marked with an "X" on his map?

Where had Tex found this rock? Would he even remember where he had found it? A lot depended on that. All this was tantalizing and exciting, but there wasn't a thing I could do about it now.

Anyway, I was getting sleepier by the moment — too sleepy to care about rock noses just now. I turned out the light and went back to bed, feeling chilly, but warming up quickly enough beneath the covers. I was so very sleepy . . . so sleepy. . . . I fell asleep with the rock nose tucked under my pillow.

And if there were any more strange sounds in the night, I didn't hear them.

The black rock was still there, pressing into my cheek, when I awoke the next morning. It felt very uncomfortable, which is probably what woke me up. The minute I touched it everything came back and I couldn't wait to be up and around—investigating. There were so many things to ask questions about, and with morning sunlight warm beyond the windows, I knew I could be smarter about getting the answers than I could in the middle of the night.

Breakfast, like everything else, was pretty informal at the Myricks'. Mr. Myrick was up early and off to his typewriter, but the rest of us seemed to straggle in when we felt like it, and if Mrs. Myrick was around, she helped us get something— or we helped ourselves. The Buddy Brothers didn't appear at all this morning. Mrs. Myrick said that being in the theatrical business, they probably stayed up late at night, and slept later than other people in the morning. I could have vouched for their being up late last night, but I didn't mention it.

Florida seemed a little more friendly than she had been, but I was so busy with the plans that were buzzing in my head that I didn't pay much attention to her. But before Tex hurried off to join his friends, I managed to catch him by himself in the hall, where only the marble Venus could overhear what I had to ask him. The rock nose bulged in a pocket of my jeans and I pulled it out and showed it to him.

"Do you remember where you found this stone?" I asked.

For once Tex didn't have to think a long while before answering. He knew every rock in his collection as though it was a personal friend.

"Sure," he said. "That's one of the rocks I found down in the glen. I told you that."

I nodded impatiently. "Yes, but *where* in the glen? Where were you when you picked up this particular rock?"

This required a little more thinking. He took the rock and turned it around a few times.

"I think I can remember," he said. "I picked this rock up one day when it started to rain. Since it was only a shower, I looked for a place to shelter in without going back to the tunnel. Some of those goblin rocks lean so far over—"

"As if they were running," I put in. "That map in the library shows a group marked 'The Frightened Sisters.' Would that be the place?"

"I think so," he said. "They slant over so far that you can crawl right under the shelter they make, when the wind is blowing from the right direction. But why is it so important, Trina? What are you up to?"

I wasn't ready to tell him yet. "Oh, I just thought I'd have a look for some rocks myself, and I might go back to where you found this one."

I don't think he believed that, but Tex wasn't one to nag a person, so he let it go. Anyway, I had what I wanted to know. This stone that looked so much like a nose had indeed been found in the place marked "X". It was all I could do not to let him see my excitement. I gave him a breezy Thanks and went to tell Mrs. Myrick I was going for a walk in the woods. That was a mistake because she promptly asked Florida to go with me.

"We can't have you getting lost in the woods, Trina," she said. "And a walk will do Florida good. She doesn't get enough exercise."

"And I eat too much," Florida added, sounding grumpy again. She was still at the kitchen table, having her fourth piece of toast and jam. She scowled at me and pushed it away from her, as though it was my fault that she had to deprive herself.

"O.K., then, come along," I said, since there was nothing else to do but accept her company.

We started off through the woods together, not talking much, and not yet really friends, in spite of listening to those records together last night. She didn't want to be with me, any more than I wanted her along, so we plodded in silence until we reached the place where we had to crawl through brush. Here she balked.

"You're not going all the way down to the glen today, are you?" she demanded.

I patted the stone in my pocket to make sure I hadn't lost

it. "Of course I am. That's what I came out for."

She looked down at her green cotton dress. "I'll scrape my knees without jeans on. And besides, Mom doesn't like rock dust ground into my clothes."

This was good news. If she chose to stay at the top, it was fine with me. "All right — you can wait for me," I said and got down to crawl through the bushes. This time my hair didn't catch because I'd done it in those bouncy side ponytails.

When I reached the cave entrance I stood for a minute breathing in the sunny air, watching a plane fly toward New York — feeling a pang of homesickness because I wasn't on it. Though not for long. Right away Florida was beside me, brushing leaves off her dress. I still hadn't lost her — so I took the next step and ducked through the entrance into the cave.

At once the air was cool and everything was brown and dim, with direct sunlight cut off. Only that slit in the rocky roof let in a faint, filtered light.

"Why are you going down?" Florida demanded, right behind me.

"Because I've got a hunch." I could tell her that much at least. In fact, by this time I wouldn't have minded telling both Florida and Tex why this stone interested me — except that I was afraid my idea was so farfetched that they would laugh at me. They might even interfere with what I wanted to do. Anyway, this morning I had no real purpose in mind except to look around and see if I could find anything this rock nose might once have belonged to. That might take a lot of looking and more than one trip.

I picked up a frayed gunnysack, shook brown dust out of it, and set it just inside the entrance to the tunnel. I was about to crawl onto it, when Florida spoke behind me.

"You'll be sorry if you go down there," she said.

I whirled around to look at her in the dim light and found that she was wearing her slightly malicious smile. All she wanted was to obstruct me, I was sure, and I knelt to crawl into the tunnel.

"If you go down, you can't get back," she said.

That was sappy—because I had already been down and I had come back. Twice. So what was to prevent me this time?

"I know how to use the ropes," I told her impatiently.

"What ropes?" she said.

This time I looked into the tunnel as I hadn't done before. In fact, I put both hands into the grooved channels at the sides and felt for the ropes. There was nothing there. No ropes at all. I crawled back out and stood up to face her angrily.

"What have you done with them?"

She widened her blue eyes at me innocently. "I haven't done anything with them. Why should I?"

"Then how did you know they're gone?"

"I can use my eyes, even if you can't," she snapped at me. "Look there! See those iron rings set in the floor? That's what the ropes are fastened to at this end. I could see right away that somebody had unknotted them and pulled the ropes off to carry them away somewhere. So if you go down to the glen this morning, there won't be any way for you to get back."

I bent to look at the rusty iron rings that someone must have sunk into the rock floor of the cave long ago. Rings that stood empty, with the rust rubbed away in the places where knotted ropes had constantly polished them. I had never even noticed them before in the dim light.

"Tex?" I questioned Florida. "Would he—"

"Of course not. He'd never pull up those ropes. Or if he did, he'd tell me and explain why."

We stared at each other in a strange, rather searching way, and a little of the irritation between us faded. There was one thing, at least, that we could agree on.

"Then it was Galvin," I said.

Florida nodded. "It must have been. He probably came here last night when he ran off while we were on the veranda. He could have come right here and taken away the ropes. It's the sort of thing he might do."

"We'll have to get more rope," I said.

"More rope for what?" asked a careless voice behind us.

Florida and I both jumped. We hadn't heard a thing, but when we turned around we found Al Buddy leaning against the rock wall at the cave's entrance, smiling at us.

"Thanks for showing me the way, girls," he said. "I decided to keep an eye on you when you started off this morning. For a city boy, I'm a good Indian tracker, don't you think? When you popped into that mess of brush and didn't come out, I decided to have a look. Thanks for showing me your secret entrance."

I couldn't say a word. I was too astonished and too annoyed. It gave me a creepy feeling to know that Al Buddy had deliberately followed us through the woods. Somehow, more and more, I began to think that Al Buddy wasn't very nice.

He bent down to look into the tunnel and he got the idea of what it was for quickly enough.

"A natural roller coaster — is that it? Very tricky. This makes everything easy, doesn't it?"

I asked him the same question I had before. "Why are you so anxious to find that money? They'd never let you keep it. You'd have to turn it over to Andrew Putney, or the town."

He looked around from his inspection of the tunnel and his smile was still in place — though it didn't look angelic anymore. It was not a smile that came from anything warm inside.

"What makes you think that?" he said. "How would anybody ever know if I found it or not? How does anybody know for sure that it hasn't already been found by someone who didn't turn it over to the town?"

It was hard to believe he could talk like that, but I had no answer for him, and he turned his smile on Florida, who didn't know it was only a fake.

"Come on, baby! If you'll tell me how to slide down that tunnel without losing most of my skin, I'll have a try at it," he said to her.

Florida melted into a disgusting eagerness to please him. "You can use that gunnysack there in the tunnel. You just lie down on it and push off. It's not hard, really, and —"

Al waited to hear no more. He crawled into the tunnel, and when Florida saw what he was about to do she began to squeal — not for his music, this time, but because of what would happen if he went down.

"Wait a minute, Al! Don't go yet! Wait—there isn't any way to—"

He was already in the tunnel and he waved a foot at her rudely. "Try and stop me!" he said.

She did her best to tell him. She opened her mouth to yell— and that was as far as she got. I don't know what possessed me, but I flew into action. I clapped my hand over her mouth so that her warning choked into a splutter. Al took off on his ride to the bottom with no heed for either of us.

Once he was on his way I pulled my hand from Florida's mouth, a little surprised that she hadn't bitten me. For a minute or two she didn't make a sound. Neither did I. We stood looking at each other and listening to the fading echoes that came out of the tunnel. When they stopped and we knew he had shot out at the bottom, we stared at each other in a sort of shocked horror. Thanks to us, Al Buddy had gone down into the glen. There he would most certainly stay until someone came with ropes to get him up again. I expected Florida to start for the house yelling for help, but, surprisingly, she didn't. We kept on staring at each other, until suddenly we both began to laugh. I think by this time she had begun to feel as I did that Al Buddy was just too smart for his own good. We laughed so hard we had trouble getting out of the cave. We were still choking with laughter as we started to crawl through the bushes.

As I went along on my hands and knees, feeling weak and silly with reaction, my eye caught something white spiked on a twig. It was a piece of paper and it looked as though it might have been caught from someone's pocket as he crawled through. Perhaps it belonged to Al, I thought, and I picked it from the bush and folded it into my pocket. I would give it to him later—when he had been rescued and wasn't feeling quite so smart.

Not until we reached the pathway home did our giggling stop. After that we walked through the woods companionably, but in a rather sober silence. Perhaps we were beginning to feel guilty, after all, even though we were pleased with ourselves.

When we came in sight of the house, Florida spoke for the first time since we left the cave.

"I don't think I really like him," she said. "I think he's up to something. And he's conceited besides."

"I know," I agreed. "After all, why would the Buddy Brothers come to perform in a little town like Camberhills, where they won't be paid nearly as much as they would get somewhere else? And why would they arrive days ahead of the festival? They don't need all that time to get ready for something like this."

"We know what they came for," Florida pointed out. "They want to have a try at treasure-hunting."

"Well, Al is having his try now," I said. "I'll bet he gets awfully sick of treasure-hunting in the next few hours."

"Will we leave him down there that long?" Florida asked doubtfully.

I was surprised to have her look to me for a decision, and I began to feel a little cocky — as though I had arranged everything that had happened all by myself.

"Let him worry for a while," I said. "Let's give him till noon, at least. That's about three hours away."

"I wish we could watch him and see what he does," Florida said. "I wish we could see him when he finds out that he's trapped. But the lookout place is too far away, and there aren't any good spots where we can see into the glen from this side."

A thought suggested by her words began to tick at the back of my mind. There was another matter I wanted to investigate anyway. But this time I would manage alone, because I wasn't sure of Florida Myrick. She seemed to take likes and dislikes too easily and suddenly.

As we crossed the grass toward the house, Joe Buddy came down the front steps and around the side in our direction. He was carrying two electric guitars in their cases. When he saw us he looked as though he might turn and run, though I couldn't imagine why. Then he set the guitars down and waited for us, gloomier than ever. Last evening he had been kind and I wished I could cheer him up.

"Thanks for playing for us last night," I said. "That was wonderful."

He looked at me and then quickly away. "I'd better tell you —" he began, but Florida interrupted with a sudden rush

of words to second my own thank-you, and he dropped whatever he meant to say.

It seemed to me that Joe was behaving in a strange way.
He was definitely uneasy, and he couldn't meet my eyes.

"Tell us what?" I urged before Florida could jump in again.

"Never mind," he said. "Have you seen Al around anywhere?"

"We saw him back there a while ago," Florida told him,
waving her hand vaguely toward the woods, not giving anything away.

"Guess I'll have to look for him," Joe said. He set the
guitars down and started off among the trees as if he was in a
hurry to get away. Something was certainly wrong, but I
couldn't figure out what—except for an uneasy feeling that it
concerned me.

Neither of us tried to stop him, though now it was my turn
to melt a little, in spite of his odd behavior. Somehow I didn't
want to play tricks on Joe Buddy. At least the path into the
woods didn't go very far, and he would soon give up. There
was no way for him to discover the hidden entrance to the cave,
and even if he shouted for Al, his voice would never carry
down into the glen.

When Florida slipped away from me and went into the
house, I wasted no time. The short way into town along the
main road would run beyond the far side of the glen. From the
road there would surely be a way up through the woods to
the house above the cliffs on the opposite side.

I started off at a brisk trot, skirting the clumps of Queen
Anne's lace that grew along the way, and noting as I hurried
that clouds were settling down all around the sky, so that the
early-morning sun had taken on a hazy look. I hoped it wouldn't
get too cloudy and dark, because I knew a place from which I
could see into the glen and find out what Al Buddy was doing
down there.

Once, as I hurried along, I patted the pocket of my jeans.
The rock that resembled Mr. Petrarch's nose was still there,
and I must not lose it. This rock was very much a part of my
future plans.

12 *The Man with the Binoculars*

I HAD no trouble finding the road that wound up the hillside off the main road to town. There were several side roads
along the way, but it was the one at the top of the hill that
interested me, and I hurried past the others, hoping the dogs
that barked at me would stay on their own grounds.

When I came to the gray house at the top, I knew it had to
be the right one because the road turned into a dead end and
went no farther. It was an old house that needed painting,
and it was not nearly as large and fine as the Putney house
in which the Myricks lived.

No one was in sight and I climbed a steep flight of stone
steps up from the road, then another flight of wooden steps
to the porch. The house was high, all right. High enough to
be above the cliffs. Its front door stood open upon a hallway
so dark that I couldn't see inside. For the first time I began to
feel uncomfortable about what I was doing. I had been hurrying along, with all my efforts bent on what I wanted to accomplish. But now, as I reached my finger toward the doorbell,
I began to think—too late, as usual.

What was I going to say to the person who came to the
door? Was I going to blurt out the fact that I had noticed
someone watching me through binoculars from this house
yesterday—and please could I borrow the glasses for a look
myself? Because that was what I wanted, though it would
certainly sound peculiar to anyone else.

The bell shrilled so loudly inside when I pushed it that I

jumped at the sound. For a second I wanted to run, as though I had been a little kid ringing forbidden doorbells. But already there was a sound of footsteps on the stairs inside, and I could only stand where I was, staring uncomfortably at the screen door.

Galvin Sewell was the last person I wanted to see. So of course it was Galvin who answered my ring. When he spied me outside on the porch he stared in surprise, not opening the screen right away.

The minute I saw him I remembered how mean he had been last night, blurting out that awful thing about my being related to Will Horst. I could feel my face getting red, but I still couldn't think of anything to say.

Galvin seemed to be struck as dumb as I was and he looked uncomfortable too. Goodness knows how long we'd have stood there regarding each other foolishly, if his sister's voice hadn't called down from upstairs.

"Who is it, Galvin? Do you want me?"

I had forgotten that a small-town library would be open only part of the time, and that Rosalie Sewell might be home.

Galvin came to life and opened the door for me, stepping back so I could come into the hall. In a moment Miss Sewell might come downstairs and I knew I had better swallow my resentment and speak to Galvin quickly.

"Al Buddy is down in the glen," I told him. "He's down there right now."

Galvin looked startled. "But how could he—I mean—"

"I know," I said impatiently. "You took away the ropes. He's down there anyway. He followed Florida and me and found out about the tunnel. And he did what I did—he went down without thinking how to get back. He's up to something, but we don't know what. So I came over here. I—I thought—"

It was my turn to come to a feeble halt, not knowing how to go on. What I had come here for was to look down into the glen myself—borrow those glasses if I could. But since I didn't know who had used them, I might be treading on dangerous ground.

Galvin went to the foot of the stairs and called up to his

sister. "It's Trina Corey," he said. "Can I bring her up to meet Gramp?"

I hadn't expected that and I backed away.

"Of course," Miss Sewell said, leaning over the rail above. "Hello, Trina. Come on up. We'd love to see you."

I tried to find my voice in order to make some excuse. How could I go upstairs and meet Mr. Putney face-to-face when he had every reason to hate the very name of Horst? I couldn't speak, and Rosalie Sewell went off along the upper hall, probably to let Mr. Putney know who was coming. Galvin turned back to me awkwardly.

"I—I'm sorry I said what I did last night. I didn't think how you might feel. I know you can't help who you are and—"

His words made my spine stiffen. "Well, thanks a lot!" I said, feeling angry again. "Maybe I'm proud of who I am, even though I'm not proud of having Will Horst for an uncle."

Galvin looked almost sheepish and I marched past him up the stairs. His sister waited for me near an open door at the rear of the hall, and I went toward her without another look at Galvin. In spite of all my hurry to come here, I was anything but prepared to meet the man Will Horst had injured so badly. As usual I hadn't figured things out ahead—I'd only figured what I wanted to do *now*. I went down the hall as slowly as I could, trying too late to prepare myself.

Miss Sewell smiled at me, as friendly as ever, and led the way into a large back bedroom, not elegantly furnished the way the guest suite was at the Putney house, but with worn, though comfortable pieces of old furniture.

Miss Sewell beckoned me toward a wide balcony that overhung the rear of the house. As I went through the door the first thing I saw was the tremendous view beyond, with the cliffs opposite and the woods and rising hills beyond. Closer at hand was Goblin Glen itself dropping away almost directly beneath the house.

With the sun pale behind a haze, and a thin mist touching the tops of pine trees on the opposite cliffs, the glen looked cold and gloomy. All the little goblin men had a black, frightening look about them and I was glad I wasn't down there.

I had no time to search for Al Buddy, however, because Mr. Putney was waiting for me.

In a wheelchair on the balcony sat a shrunken old man with a rim of white hair around his bald head. I would never have recognized him as the handsome, forceful Andrew Putney of the portrait — except, perhaps, for his eyes. In spite of the wrinkles that ranged from the outer corners, and lids that drooped a little, he regarded me with the same assured look of the portrait. I winced before this look, wondering how I had dared to come to a place where I could be so little welcome.

From among the folds of blankets wrapped about him, Mr. Putney fumbled a bony hand into the open and held it out to me.

"Come here, child," he said. "Let me look at you. So you are Fred Horst's great-granddaughter? How fine that you've come back to Camberhills!"

Surprise set me staring, wide-eyed. I wanted to give Galvin a triumphant look, but I couldn't take my fascinated gaze away from the thin, wrinkled face of the man in the wheelchair. When I held out my hand, he took it with a surprisingly firm grip and drew me close so that he could peer up into my face.

"You don't look much like the rest of the family," he said. "Except for that red hair. All the Horsts had red hair. Did you know that? I could see your hair when I watched you yesterday through my glasses. Didn't take you long to get down there, did it? How do you like our Goblin Glen?"

He went so fast he took my breath away. He might be old and ill, but there was nothing wrong with his wits, and he wasn't holding Will Horst against me.

"I saw your glasses shining in the sun," I admitted. "I thought it was Galvin watching me."

He smiled thinly from his nest of blankets and shook his head. "I've watched people hunt for treasure down there for a good many years. Since I can't hunt any longer myself, I watch the others. In the beginning none of us knew where to look. The whole place, even the caves in the cliffs and the stream bed, were fair ground for hunting. But nothing turned up. There were too many places to search. So either we missed the hiding place, or somebody came back who knew his way and got the money out on some dark night. That's what most people believe—but I've always had a feeling in my bones that it's still there and that we missed out, somehow. Though I suppose we'll never know now. I'd like to have had the answer before I die. I'd like to have paid some of that money back."

He closed his eyes and sank into the coverings he needed to keep the chill away, although it was a warm day. I had a choked feeling in my throat as I looked at him, and a sudden understanding of why Galvin wanted so much to help this old man who was his great-grandfather.

Miss Sewell leaned over and gently tucked in an edge of blanket. "Let us know when you're tired," she said, "and we'll get you back to bed."

Galvin had stepped to the balcony rail and was looking down into the glen with the old man's glasses. "I wonder what that long-haired nut is doing down there," he muttered.

There had been a time when I would have bristled to hear anyone call Al Buddy a "long-haired nut," but now I was less sensitive. I went to stand curiously beside Galvin. Even without glasses I could see the glen much more clearly from this balcony than I had been able to from the lookout rock with Mr. Myrick. Because the sunlight was so thin and hazy, there were no shadows down there and I could make out the figure of Al Buddy easily. He stood up tall among The Frightened Sisters and as I watched he bent over something and then straightened again.

I gave Galvin a startled poke with my elbow. "How did he know how to go to the right place? How could he have seen the map in the library?" I looked at Miss Sewell. "Has Al Buddy come to the library since he has been in town? Or his brother?"

She shook her head. "Neither of them has been there. I'm on duty when the library is open, so I can promise you I'd know if they were there."

Mr. Putney looked up from his nest. "The map has never been a secret," he pointed out. "We put it on display soon after we received it. As soon as we found that it didn't help us, we put it out where others could see it, in case someone else could figure out what it meant. Anyone might know about it. This boy could have learned of it through other people before he came here."

"He—he looks as if he's building something," Galvin said, sounding puzzled.

I had to look through those glasses for myself. "Please let me see," I begged him.

He handed me the glasses and stood by while I focused them and stared down into the glen. Everything leaped toward me, tremendously magnified. I found myself looking at The Witch's Sons as though they were practically in my lap. I had to move the glasses around a bit before I found Al Buddy.

What Galvin said was true. He seemed to be building up a pile of rocks down there—almost as if he were making an extra goblin in the place where Old Beak Nose was supposed to be. But for what purpose?

From his chair Mr. Putney spoke again. "Even when Will Horst's daughter sent us the map twenty years later, it did us no good because there never was one of those rock figures that answered to the description of Old Beak Nose. The map was either a hoax, or we never knew how to read it."

He sighed deeply and Rosalie Sewell stepped toward him, anxious lest he tire himself. My mind was going a mile a minute off in a new direction. Carefully I drew the stone Tex had given me from my pocket and held it out on my palm.

"Tex Myrick collects rocks," I said. "He found this one near the very place that is marked with an 'X' on the map."

Galvin took the glasses from me and put them down. He was staring at the black chunk of rock in my hand. Miss Sewell looked at it too, and Mr. Putney reached out for it. I gave it to him without a word and he turned it round and round as I had done, looking at it from every side. He ran a thin finger over the curve of the beak, and then looked at the two dents that seemed like nostrils underneath.

"It's rather like a nose, isn't it?" he said thoughtfully.

I was glad he saw that too. "Like a beaked nose!" I cried.

"So what?" Galvin said.

Mr. Putney's lower lip folded over his upper one, and his shaggy white eyebrows drew down in a frown of concentration. We all kept still, watching him.

"I've had plenty of time to think during these last few years," he said. "And the only conclusion I've been able to come to is that there must have been a beak-nosed goblin rock down there at one time. We wouldn't have noticed it in the days when we didn't know about the map. Twenty years later, when the map came to us, there was no such figure to be seen. What could have happened to it? Is this stone all that is left of Old Beak Nose?" The old man made a sudden movement in his chair. "If only I could get down to the glen! If only —"

Galvin shook his head. "It wouldn't do any good, Gramp. You know I've never stopped looking down there."

"I know that, boy," the old man said. "Yet you never found this stone."

"Because it doesn't mean anything by itself," Galvin protested. "All that rock down there is solid, except for some loose stuff, and I've moved around everything that's loose dozens of times. Nothing was ever hidden under the loose pieces. And you can't move the rest unless you blasted, or broke it up with a sledgehammer. Will Horst and Burt Boyd certainly never did that."

I took back the nose stone, unwilling to believe what Galvin was saying. "All the same, this means something. I know it does. It has to mean something. It can't be just a coincidence."

Mr. Putney gave me his thin, frail smile, but Galvin merely grunted and put the glasses to his eyes again.

"What I don't understand is why these Buddy Boys are so interested in trying to find that money," he said. "Even if they found it, and even though it amounted to quite a lot, it wouldn't be as much as they can earn in a year. They must make more money than that in a year, easily."

Mr. Putney closed his eyes in distress at the idea of young boys making so much money by plunking on guitars.

"But they are going to stop making money soon," I said. "Joe wants to break up the team and go to college, and Al can't prevent him. So Al wants to get a whole lot of money ahead and—"

Miss Sewell shook her head. "Galvin is right, Trina. It can't mean that much to them. I expect all young people are interested in treasure, and perhaps these two boys haven't had much real adventure in their lives. Besides, if they found anything, it would be wonderful publicity in their line of work."

I didn't argue, because I wasn't all that interested in Al and Joe Buddy right then. The idea at the back of my mind was urging me into action and I turned anxiously to Miss Sewell.

"When will the library be open again? I'd like to have another look at that map," I said.

Galvin snorted impolitely, but his sister seemed to understand.

"Take Trina down to the library and let her in," she said to her brother. "There's no reason why she shouldn't see the map if she wants to. I won't be there to open up till two this afternoon, when Mrs. Birch comes to look after Gramp."

Galvin started to snort again, but he must have remembered what he had done to me last night, because he suddenly relented.

"All right," he said, and handed the glasses to his great-grandfather. "Maybe you'd better keep an eye on what's going on down in the glen."

This time Miss Sewell moved quickly and intercepted the binoculars. "No, dear. That's enough excitement for this morning. Gramp is tired, and I want you to help me get him back to bed before you go. No more glen-watching now."

So that was the way it was managed. When Mr. Putney, who really was too tired to protest, had been helped back to bed, Galvin and I started downtown to the library.

At least Galvin was more friendly now, and while we didn't have much to say to each other, he came along willingly enough.

The garage that had once been Fred Horst's livery stable was the first building we passed as we reached Main Street, and through its open front I saw the garage men I'd seen yesterday. The one working on the Buddy Brothers' car looked up as we passed and seemed to recognize me.

"Hi, there," he said, giving me a wide smile. "Why didn't you tell me who you are when you were in here yesterday?"

I came to an abrupt halt on the sidewalk, and Galvin stopped beside me. A warning prickle seemed to start at the back of my neck and moved upward to my scalp.

"What do you mean?" I asked cautiously.

His grin grew wider under the smears of grease across his face. "Why—that you're the great-granddaughter of Fred Horst, who used to own this place."

"H-how did you know?" I asked in a very faint voice.

He called to his assistant across the garage. "Hey, Mike— show her the paper. It's all there in a big write-up. All about you being in town and about how your mother's name is Horst. That makes you the great-niece of our famous bank robber, doesn't it?"

The man named Mike brought the newspaper, but Galvin

had to take it from him because I felt too limp to pick it up. Galvin spread it open to the front page, and sure enough, there it was in a big headline: HORST DESCENDANT VISITS CAMBERHILLS. There was my name in print: TRINA COREY, and the fact that I was visiting the Myricks. Everything was there to identify me. I couldn't even be angry, I felt so awful. I simply gave Galvin a blurry look and started to walk away.

He flung the paper down and came after me. "Look, Trina— I didn't tell Bill Eckers—or anybody else. Honestly, I didn't."

I couldn't care less who had told. All I wanted was to get to the library and hide as quickly as possible. Will Horst had practically ruined Camberhills. People he had injured were still alive, and so were many of their descendants. And now everyone was going to stare at me, and snicker behind my back, and wonder if bad blood like that was inherited. They would wonder how I dared show my face in this town. And of course they would say I had tried to keep my identity a secret—as I really had.

Galvin opened the library door and I hurried inside to a safe, protective world of books. If only I were reading a book now—so that I could know I was safe, no matter what happened to the people in the story.

When he had closed the door behind us and turned on the fan to move the warm, dead air, Galvin folded his arms like a policeman and stood in front of me.

"You have to believe I didn't do this," he said. "I know what I said last night when I was sore at you, but I was glad the whole thing was stopped before the man from the newspaper came."

"Only it wasn't stopped," I said.

Galvin had no answer for that. He swung away from me across the room to the glass display cabinet where the old map was kept, and when he turned his back I fumbled in my pocket for a handkerchief. I didn't want to cry, but I was afraid I was going to.

Instead of a handkerchief I pulled a folded square of paper from my pocket and stared at it blankly. It seemed to be a ruled sheet torn from a notebook, and it looked shabby and worn at the creases. I couldn't think for a minute where it could have come from and I began to unfold it slowly, blinking my eyes hard to hold back the tears. Then, quite suddenly, I remembered.

This was the scrap of paper I had found caught on a twig in the underbrush when Florida and I had crawled back to the path after leaving Al Buddy in the glen. Some marks had been made on the paper—rather crude drawings in pencil that had smudged and faded a little. The paper seemed ready to fall apart in my hands and I carried it carefully to the front of the library where gray daylight came through the windows. I caught my breath as I studied it.

This, too, was a plan of the glen. But it was very crude and rough, without much detail drawn in. The one clear drawing on the paper was that of a single goblin. A goblin with a smooth, egg-shaped head, and a great curving beak of a nose!

Al Buddy did indeed know where to look and what for. However he had come by this sheet of paper, the one comforting thing was that I still had that rocklike nose in my pocket. If that was what he was looking for down there, he wasn't going to find it.

13 *The Fake Goblin*

I MUST have shouted without knowing it, because Galvin turned from the glass case and stared at me. I waved the paper at him wildly.

"Come and look!" I cried. "Come quickly and look!"

When I had spread the paper out carefully on a table and explained where I had found it, we pored over it together. Someone had lettered a few words under the goblin figure and Galvin read them aloud in astonishment: "OLD FAKE BEAK NOSE."

"What does it mean?" I asked. I had forgotten all about crying. I couldn't worry about being the most notorious character in town now. What we saw before us was too exciting.

"It means that Gramp is right," Galvin said. "There actually was another figure in the glen at some time or other."

"But what does the word 'fake' mean in connection with it?" I wondered.

"I don't know, except that maybe somebody built an extra figure in that spot where the 'X' is marked on the other map. This isn't a map, really—it's more like a diagram."

I bent close to study the blurred markings, and now I saw something else. The goblin drawing seemed to be made up of four segments, separated by dotted lines.

"Maybe the word 'fake' is just to show that it wasn't a real rock goblin," I said. "And the dotted lines are to show where it was put together."

"You could be right." Galvin leaned closer. "And that solid

OLD FAKE BEAK NOSE

line near the bottom is the ground. So—"

"So the money was hidden in a hole under the base stone!" I broke in, very excitedly. "That's what the lines at the bottom mean—a hole. In the time they were down there those two robbers must have built a fake goblin to mark the place where they hid the money."

"Sure, sure, sure!" Galvin said impatiently. "Only there aren't any holes there. Do you think I haven't scraped off the earth that has gathered around those figures right down to bedrock?"

I fumbled in my pocket for the nose rock and brought it out, paying no attention to Galvin's objections. The stone seemed to match the nose in the picture. But I was more interested now in the flat part where the rock might have been stuck onto the egg-shaped head of the figure.

"Look," I said, scraping at something with my fingernail.

Galvin took the stone from me and as he picked at the grayish remnants that clung to it, his face brightened. "Clay!" he said. "That would do it. There's a layer of clay down there in a bank above the stream. The Indians around here used to make their pots from it. Will Horst would have known it was there."

"But clay that wasn't fired wouldn't last very long, would it?" I asked.

"Maybe they didn't expect it to last. Maybe they expected to get back quickly and get the money out. In the meantime nobody would ever notice one more goblin shape among all the rest. Only those two were caught right away and they never returned at all. And after a while the clay that held the pieces together dried out, so that any storm could blow the figure over and break it apart."

This all sounded possible. "If that's what happened, the base stone must still be there," I said. "With the money under it. That's what the drawing seems to show."

Galvin shook his head gloomily and repeated his previous words. "There isn't any base stone. There isn't any hollow like the one in the drawing."

"Then something's wrong," I said. "Something has to be wrong."

There were sounds out on the street where several teen-age boys and girls were going by. I stood up to look and Galvin went to the door.

"They're heading for the meetinghouse," he said. "There's supposed to be a festival rehearsal this morning. That's our local group going past. They're pretty good, too. They've won a few contests around the country. Come along and let's see what's going on."

I folded the diagram carefully and put it in one pocket of my jeans, with the rock nose in the other. I couldn't be interested in the festival right now, and I didn't want to go out in a crowd under the circumstances.

"Don't you think we should go back to the glen and have another look?" I said.

"With old Buddy-buddy down there?" Galvin shook his head.

I had practically forgotten about Al. "He can't get out unless you put the ropes back," I reminded Galvin. "Don't you think —"

"Later," Galvin said. "Come along to the meetinghouse first."

I hung back. "I don't want to go over there. Everyone will know who I am, and—"

Galvin looked exasperated. "All right—so you're famous! What do you care? What does it matter?"

"It's not a pleasant way to be famous," I said. "I'll hate it if people stare and point and—"

"They won't," Galvin snapped. "They'll only be interested. Nobody is going to blame you for what Will Horst did forty years ago. You've got everything mixed up, so it makes no sense."

I looked at him coldly. *"You* blamed me. You hated me the minute you saw me. Just because my great-uncle was Will Horst."

Galvin blinked a couple of times—and then he smiled. He really smiled at me for the first time. It was surprising how nice and how friendly he could look when he smiled.

"I guess I had things pretty mixed up too," he admitted. "Maybe I had a few mixed-up ideas of my own about what you wanted to do with that money if you ever found it."

I couldn't stay mad. I had to smile at him. "If you want to know," I said sheepishly, "I made up a dream in my head about what I would do if I was the one to find that money. I made up a story about being on the platform during the festival, with Mr. Davidson introducing me as the person who had done what nobody else ever managed to do. I was going to be up on that platform making a fine speech that everyone would applaud. And then I'd turn over the lost money to you and your sister and your great-grandfather. That's all I ever wanted to do with it. So now you can laugh your head off, if you like."

He didn't laugh. His dark eyes regarded me with new kindness and no mockery. I remembered the time I had seen him making speeches among the goblins. Galvin Sewell would understand about make-believe dreams.

"I've done that sort of thing too," he said, "—though I've never told anyone before. I've even pretended I was a selectman of this town. I'd like to do something for Camberhills that would make Putney an honored name again, instead of just the name of a man whose bank failed and ruined a lot of people. I guess that's why I hate some of the things Mr. Davidson is doing. I don't know if they're really good for the town. Anyway, come along, Trina, and let's see what's going on at the meetinghouse."

We went together down the street and there was a good feeling between us that had never been there before. Now Galvin was my friend. For the first time we trusted each other. He had made everything a little better for me, in spite of what he had blurted out last night, in spite of that awful write-up in the paper. And perhaps I had made some things a little better for him. We were in this together — to solve the mystery of Goblin Glen, to find an answer. I couldn't help feeling that we had come a little closer to a solution.

Not until we reached the walk in front of the meetinghouse did the big question hit me. All around us boys and girls from town were milling about, wanting to watch the rehearsal, and the town policeman was out keeping an eye on things. No one paid any attention to me and I came to a stop, grabbing Galvin by the arm.

"However in the world did Al Buddy come to have that diagram of Old Beak Nose?" I asked.

Galvin seemed to think this wasn't important. "Who knows how many hands that piece of paper has passed through since it was first made. You can't even be sure it was Al who lost it in the bushes. You're just leaping to a conclusion. Come on — I know how to get inside the meetinghouse."

We bypassed the crowd of kids milling around the town square out in front and Galvin led the way to a basement door. The janitor was a friend of his and when we explained that we knew the Buddy Brothers, he let us in. A few moments later we stood against a side wall in the auditorium where we could watch what was happening.

On the stage the town combo was setting up its drums and a small electric organ, arranging amplifiers and loudspeakers. There were electric wires all over the place, and two boys with bright-red guitars were strumming away in a quick practice session. The noise was tremendous, with each boy apparently trying out his instrument without paying much attention to the others.

Down on the floor, in the space between the first row of seats and the platform, Mr. Davidson—looking a little dazed—was talking to a woman who Galvin said was the high school music teacher, and director of the festival besides. I thought she looked dazed too, as though the sounds from the platform were giving her a headache. A third man, whom Galvin didn't know, was talking to the other two, and when Mr. Davidson saw Galvin and me, he gestured in our direction. In the front rows sat other young people who were here for the festival, all talking and sometimes yelling at one another, which added to the uproar.

Then, as some signal was given, the boys on the platform got together and began their first number. A boy of about seventeen stepped up to the center mike and began to accompany his own singing. His was the solo voice and he was doing one of the Beatles' songs. For a few minutes I forgot about Galvin and the glen and everything else. The sound was much louder than on television. It blasted through the big hall, and the beat was there—the great big beat that kids like to listen to, and most grown-ups can't understand. Maybe that was one of the reasons we liked it—because it was *our* music. It was young and it was saying—in a very loud voice—all the things we sometimes felt like saying and couldn't. But folk music it certainly wasn't.

"Let's get out of here!" Galvin shouted in my ear. Apparently it wasn't *his* music.

Before we could leave, the stranger who had been talking to Mr. Davidson came over to us, took us each by the elbow, and propelled us through the nearest doorway into the hall.

"Even though I make my living out of that sound," he said, "there are times when I like to hear myself think. Mr. Davidson says you may know where I can find Al and Joe. I'm their manager, and I've come up from New York on a business matter. Besides that, they're supposed to be here this morning getting their own show set up."

"I—I think we can find them," I said, not looking at Galvin.

"It may take a little while, though."

He gave me a quick pat on the shoulder. "Hop to it, young lady." He moved away as though everything was settled, and then turned back. "Oh, yes—when you see them, tell the Boyds that Jim Harvester is here."

Galvin and I had started off, but we did a double take and turned back so fast we bumped into each other.

"Who did you say?" Galvin asked.

"Jim Harvester—they'll know—"

This time I was faster than Galvin. "Not *your* name. The other name—the other name you said!"

My excitement must have startled him. "You mean the *Boyds?* That's their real name. You didn't think they were born with a name like Buddy, did you? Though they stick to Buddy for public use."

Neither Galvin nor I said a word. We turned around and tore for the basement stairs. We let ourselves out the side door and slipped away. Without any argument we knew we were heading for Goblin Glen. And this time it was a real live goblin that had suddenly turned up in the town of Camberhills.

"Boyd!" Galvin repeated as we hurried along. "The Buddy Brothers are related to —"

"To Burt Boyd!" I broke in. "Will Horst's partner. What sneaky crooks they are! Of all the awful—"

"Come on," Galvin said, "we've got to hurry."

As though we weren't already hurrying as fast as we could go. I was puffing and out of breath by the time we had climbed the hill. Fortunately Galvin knew a shortcut through the woods, so we didn't need to go near the Putney house.

When we reached the tunnel entrance, he brought out the ropes he had hidden, and we went into the cave together. Al was still down there in the glen. He had to be there. No one could get out without these ropes. Galvin knotted them into their rings and flung the coils down the tunnel. Then he picked up a gunnysack from the pile and dived in ahead of me. I followed right away, though I felt a little dizzy and battered by this time. First by the sounds of that crazy beat music back in the hall, and then from the way the name Boyd was making a loud beating sound inside my head. As if it kept time to "How Do I Get Along?"

The slide down the tunnel ended with a whoosh as I shot out on the grassy bank above the glen. Galvin was already standing, looking around. For the first time I realized how misty the morning had grown. When I had looked down from Mr. Putney's balcony a while ago, mist had touched the tops of the pines, but now it crept in little wreaths and swirls among the goblin rocks. The Witch's Sons looked more wicked than ever, standing up black in the swirling mist. I was suddenly glad not to be here alone. Galvin knew his way around this place, if anyone did.

"I don't see him, do you?" Galvin said.

The central group of goblins was hazy—The Frightened Sisters seemed to be running through the mist. But anyone who stood up among them would have been easy to see. It could be that Al was crouching behind the rocks, as Galvin had done the first time I had visited the glen.

Galvin didn't wait for the shake of my head, but started off. I trailed after him, not too sure of my footing over the rock-strewn bed of the glen. Galvin was sure every inch of the way, and he led us straight to the running figures of that group marked "X." We climbed up into the midst of the Sisters, but Al Buddy—Boyd—was not there!

As we already knew, he had been here earlier, and now we could see what he had built. The diagram had been his, all right—probably handed down in the Boyd family for years—and he had re-created a figure that was almost exactly like the drawing in the diagram. Except for two missing parts. The nose wasn't there, and neither was the base stone. He had set a squarish rock resembling the body of the figure on the space of earth in the heart of the group, and had balanced the egg-shaped stone on top of it. The head was a rounded stone that might have been carried up here from the stream bed long ago.

I took the nose rock from my pocket and handed it to Galvin. He examined the "head" carefully and found a place where old scraps of rough clay still clung. When he held the nose to the face of it, we knew it belonged there. More rough bits of clay clung to the base of the head, and to the body stone where the head rested. But when Galvin gave the whole thing a good shove it toppled over and fell apart. There was certainly nothing underneath it. Nor was either stone hollow.

"Why did he build it up like that?" I asked, more puzzled than ever.

Galvin shrugged. "Maybe just to get an idea of how it must have looked. Maybe to find out if he was in the right place. The important thing now is where has Al gone?"

He stood up, cupped his hands around his mouth, and shouted Al's name several times. The echoes went barking back and forth around the glen from cliff to rocky cliff, but there was no answer from Al. And with mist rolling in all around, the far reaches of the glen were no longer visible.

I kicked at one of the rocks at my feet. "You don't suppose he could have found—" I began.

Galvin looked at the space of shallow, rocky earth that had collected among the goblin rocks, sifting in over the years. It seemed that Al had been trying to dig up the weedy earth in a haphazard sort of way, but the bedrock underneath showed through and he must have given up the effort.

"I'm going to look for him," Galvin said.

I jumped up to go with him. I didn't want to be left alone in this place of goblins, with someone whose name was Boyd moving around unseen, perhaps watching us.

"You stay here, Trina," Galvin said. "Then you can call if he comes back. I'll take a quick look around the glen and over where the rock heap starts at the cut."

Galvin was so newly my friend that I didn't want to tell him I was afraid to stay here alone. I let him go, and he jumped down from among the rock goblins and started off through the glen. In moments the mist had swirled in to hide him from me. It seemed to deaden sound so that in a few minutes I could no longer hear him moving among the rocks. Even the bulldozer was quiet today—perhaps because of the weather.

Somehow it was uncomfortable to stand up in clear view, aware of all the ugly figures around me, and in plain sight of

anyone who popped out of the mist to catch me here. As soon as I could no longer hear Galvin I crouched down beneath slanting rocks that made a sort of roof high over my head. Now and then I peered out from between cracks in the rock, but I could no longer see the tunnel. Overhead there was only a thick white covering of mist that thinned here or rolled thicker there, but with no glimmer of sunshine coming through. If old Mr. Putney was out on his balcony, he wouldn't be able to see a thing through his glasses.

Somewhere not far away I heard a click, as if a small stone had rolled against another, and my heart began to thump. It was an awful feeling, knowing that a Boyd was hiding somewhere in this place. Of course he must be hiding. Otherwise he would have answered Galvin's call. My fearful thoughts began to mix Al Buddy up with Burt Boyd. People said Burt had been the criminal brains behind not only the bank robbery but other serious robberies in the area. Burt, who had died violently in a fight in prison! This was a place of old wickedness, I thought, shivering. All I wanted was to get out of here and never come back.

What if Al was watching me right now? What if he knew perfectly well that I was here alone and—

I said, "Silly—silly—silly!" under my breath several times very fast, and tried to make myself think of other things.

The long-lost money, for instance. What had Tex said about finding the stone that looked like a nose? He had taken shelter from rain under some slanting rocks here among The Frightened Sisters. Rocks that had made a roof to protect him. Like the rocks that reached over my head. They slanted up quite high, and curved over a little so that the place was almost like an open cave. From above, the slant of the rocks made this group of figures look as if they reached out their arms as they ran.

If the nose stone had fallen here, could it be that the original figure had stood very near this spot? If Old Beak Nose had been built under the shelter of this slanting rock roof, he would hardly have been noticed from outside by the early searchers for the money. Or if they had seen him, they would have taken him to be another goblin. And by the time the Horst family sent the map to Mr. Putney, the figure would have toppled over, with its pieces scattered. No one would have looked for a "fake" goblin.

But suppose — just suppose — Suddenly I began to scrabble about the weedy patches of earth, trying to find a flat stone I might dig with. When I found one that would do, I began to scrape away the earth beneath the slanting rocks. It wasn't very deep and in a few minutes I was down to the rock base. Only this time I didn't stop. What if it wasn't the real base, after all?

Feverishly I worked at the earth, shoving it away, scraping until I had a bald patch of rock uncovered. Then I knelt and put my hands upon it, leaned on the rock with my full weight. I couldn't be sure, but it seemed as though there was a hint of a teeter under my hands — as if this rock was not as solid as the rest of the pile. As long as there was earth on top, it was packed in firmly — but now I wasn't so sure.

It seemed to be a large, flat rock and I couldn't dig it out by myself. If this was really Old Beak Nose's base stone, then it was too big for me to handle. I jumped up and cupped my hands about my mouth as Galvin had done and shouted for him with all my might.

From some distant place out there in the mist I heard him answer, "Coming!" and I shouted again so that he would hurry. Of course he thought I had found Al, and he came leaping across the rocks and up to where I knelt under the ledge of rock.

"Where is he?" Galvin demanded.

"I don't know where Al is, and I don't much care," I said. "Look, Galvin! See if you think this rock moves a little when you put your weight on it."

He got the idea right away, and stepped onto the bare place I had cleared, bending over to miss the roof ledge. I couldn't tell whether he felt any movement or not, but when he turned to look at me his eyes were dark and shining.

"If only we had something good to dig with," I said.

"Do you think I don't have?" He clambered off among the

rocks and in a moment he was back with a rusty shovel he had hidden for digging use.

He went to work at once, shoveling away more of the earth cover, trying to find an edge to the stone that had moved. If there was an edge, it would mean this stone was separate from the rock base. He wasn't long in finding the rim. The stone had been set carefully in place so that its edge almost matched the real bedrock. As he pried the spade beneath it, the stone teetered unwillingly. I added my weight to the spade handle and the big rock began to stir and grind a little — as though we were waking it from a long sleep. A sleep that had lasted for forty years!

Near these particular rock goblins, who reached their arms above our heads, the bedrock slanted into a hollow — a dish-shaped space that had been covered for years by the rock that must once have made the base for Old Beak Nose. After the top part of the figure had fallen over and been scattered, wind and rain must have covered the rock with earth until it looked exactly like the rest of the bedrock down here. By the time people came deliberately to look among The Frightened Sisters, there was no telling it from the rest. Only now we knew it was an individual rock.

As we heaved and levered with the spade, the big flat rock finally came loose with a loud plopping sound and Galvin managed to push it away from the hollow underneath. Then he flung the spade aside and we both dropped to our knees to look into the shallow hole. The flat packet that lay there was black with earth. All sorts of little bug things were scurrying madly away from the light that had been let in upon their hiding place.

I didn't want to reach in among those crawly things, and I sat back while Galvin pulled out the big flat parcel and dusted it free of bugs and earth.

"It was wrapped in oilcloth, so it's been well protected," Galvin said, and I heard the tremble of excitement in his voice.

"Well, open it — open it!" I cried, and the words came out practically in a screech.

Galvin reached toward the top flap of the packet and then stopped. "No," he said. "You found it, Trina. You figured it out. Go ahead and unwrap it."

I didn't hesitate. I reached out with both hands and fumbled the packet open. My fingers were shaking, but I managed to spread the stiff oilcloth flaps apart—and there it was! There it all was—where it had lain hidden for forty years.

The money seemed to be in large old-fashioned bills. And the gold was there too. Stacks and stacks of gold coins, as well as a small bag that probably held silver.

We knelt side by side, staring at the miracle. I know there was a lump in my throat that made it hard for me to swallow, and I knew that Galvin was choked with feeling too. Even though he couldn't say a word, I knew he must be thinking of his great-grandfather and what the finding of this money, the solving of the old mystery, would mean to him.

The voice that broke in on us had a mocking ring. It came from directly behind us and we scrambled around to see Al Buddy standing there, watching us. His eyes were feverishly bright, and he was smiling in that way I didn't like.

"Thanks for doing the job for me, kids," he said. "Now if you'll just move out of my way—"

Neither of us stirred. Galvin started to speak, but he stopped when Al leaned over and calmly picked up the shovel, holding it like a club in his hands.

"You heard me," he said. "Get out of the way!"

A Boyd had come back to Goblin Glen.

14 *A Jangle for Trina Corey*

THERE was nothing for Galvin and me to do but get up from our knees and stand aside so that Al could lean over the open packet. He kept an eye on us as he did so, however, so there was no chance for Galvin to get behind him, or for me to snatch away that shovel, even if I'd dared try.

"Well, what do you know!" Al said softly. "It's been waiting here all these years. For you and me to find, Trina—left by Will Horst and Burt Boyd. Even the kid here—Galvin—and his great-grandfather the banker. We're all tied together in putting it here and digging it out."

He leaned over with a single swift movement and picked up the little bag of silver. I felt so sick that I didn't dare to look at Galvin. This would be terrible for him—to see Al take all this away, right from under our eyes.

"You'll never get away with it," Galvin growled. "You're crazy if you think you can. That money belongs to Camber-hills. And the minute you start cashing in those old bills the police will pick you up. Besides, it's against the law to have gold in your possession these days."

Al grinned at him, backing away a little, so he had both of us in front of him again.

"Sure," he said. "I know that. So you don't need to worry, do you? Maybe all I'm after is the publicity—a good story, with Al Buddy the hero. Ever think of that? I thought of it, Trina, when I called up that newspaper fellow after he left last night and tipped him off about you being a Horst.

So he could make his story a lot better."

So Al was the one who had talked! I might have guessed. I remembered the way Joe had started to tell me something when we'd met a while ago, and then had stopped. Had Joe known? Had he been ashamed of what his brother had done? I didn't know. I'd never been able to figure Joe out.

But Galvin shrugged Al's words aside. "You're just blowing up smoke screens so we'll let you get away with this. But you won't. I told you—"

"Cool it, kid," Al said. "That's enough. Now you two climb down from this pile of rock and start for the tunnel. But don't go too fast—I'm coming right after you. I'd like to know how you get out of this place. Pretty smart, weren't you, Trina—shunting me off down here?"

Several wild ideas flashed through my mind as I climbed down from among The Frightened Sisters. If Galvin and I dashed off in different directions in the mist, Al wouldn't be able to follow us both and we could play a horrible sort of hide-and-seek with him down here. Though he would probably give up soon and go back to the tunnel. And then he'd see the ropes and realize how he could get to the top. Once up there ahead of us, nothing would prevent him from pulling them up, just as Galvin had, leaving us stranded. He could be out of town and a long way off before the alarm was sounded. Perhaps he even had some special plan for getting away from the country and taking the money with him.

These thoughts took no more than a flash of time as Galvin and I climbed toward The Witch's Sons. I was sure Galvin was thinking with all his might too, trying to find a way out. If only the sun were shining so old Mr. Putney could be out on his balcony with his binoculars—but when I looked that way, all I could see was thick mist. The tops of the cliffs were not in sight, and the lookout rock, from which I had first seen the glen, was completely invisible.

We reached the foot of the sloping bank to the tunnel's entrance, and I thought of making a run for it and starting up before Al could do the same thing. If I could reach the top first and—

It was right then that something astonishing happened. I could see the tunnel opening now, and as I looked up the bank toward it, I heard a clatter of sound that was familiar. Galvin looked too, as Chipper shot out of the tunnel and came barking delightedly to meet us. Sounds told me the others were behind him, and a moment later Tex came out in a long dive, riding a gunnysack. And then came Florida Myrick. Never could I have imagined being so glad to see Florida and Tex.

I started to sputter warnings to them, but before I could make myself clear, the last of the tunnel riders shot into view — Joe Buddy! He arrived on the grass and pulled himself uncertainly to his feet. Would Joe be on Al's side? Could four kids like us outwit and defeat the two Buddy-Boyd brothers?

"We've been looking for you everywhere!" Florida cried to Al — as though she hadn't known where he was all along. "Your manager is here from New York and he wants to see you right away. Besides, there's a rehearsal going on and — "

Al paid no attention to her. "What do you think?" he said to his brother. "Young Trina here has found the lost money from the Putney Bank."

Joe looked at Galvin, then at me. "Is that true?"

"It's true, all right," Galvin told him gloomily. "Your brother thinks he can get away with what belongs to Camberhills."

Joe turned slowly toward Al, not saying anything. He'd left his dark glasses behind, and the expression in his eyes was a little frightening. I didn't know what it meant. I was going to hate it if Joe Buddy turned out to be as awful as his brother.

"This kid's off his rocker," Al said.

That was when I really looked at Al for the first time since we had started toward the tunnel. He had dropped the shovel beside him and was holding out his empty hands — where I had expected to see him carrying the packet of money.

"What would I want with that bank loot?" he asked his brother, and the angelic smile that I distrusted was in place again. "I only wanted the fun of finding it, and the publicity. You know that, Joe. It's back there where we left it, and the kids can take it home to old Putney whenever they want."

Florida began to ask a storm of questions and Tex told her curtly to keep quiet. What mattered most now was what Joe did, and whose side he was on. His look shifted to me and I knew he was again questioning his brother's words.

"Is this true?" he repeated.

I could only admit that Al seemed to be speaking the truth. Obviously he didn't have the packet with him. It was too large to conceal.

"All he picked up was a little sack of silver," I told Joe. "So I guess it's all back there. But the way he acted, we — we — thought — "

Joe held out his hand. "Better give it here, Al," he said quietly.

Al began to back away. The smile was gone and his eyes had a cold threat in them.

"Stay away!" he warned his brother, and quick as a flash he had picked up that wicked-looking shovel again.

Joe hesitated and Al held up the shovel. "I told you I didn't take anything that belongs to the town. It's all back there. You can go and see. The bank will have a record. Unless Burt and Will took out something in their pockets when they tried to escape, you'll find every cent of the money there. Now get out of my way!"

Al's full attention was on Joe, and Galvin saw our chance. With his hands close to his sides he made a slight, scattering motion. I saw it and so did Tex and we began to move backward on the grass, each in a different direction, away from Joe and Al. Florida saw the gesture too, and for once she did the right thing. She moved toward Al with a skipping motion that distracted his attention.

"How wonderful that you've found all that money!" she cried, making him look at her, and away from us, away from Joe. At the same moment Chipper suddenly decided that he didn't like Al Buddy one bit. With furious yaps he darted at his feet and Al jumped back, forgetting us completely.

I was about to dash off into the mist and try to circle toward the tunnel, when Tex took action of his own. He slipped

around behind Al, rushed him suddenly, and grabbed at his jacket before Al knew what was happening. When Tex sprang away, he held up the little bag that I thought had silver in it.

Al swung around too late. Joe closed in on him from the side and there was a scuffle in which the shovel went flying. Then the brothers were rolling over and over in frightening rough-and-tumble combat. Al struck at his brother again and again, but Joe was the wiry one, and he managed to duck and come out on top. At some point or other he got a good hold on his brother, just the way wrestlers do on television—and Al was pinned to the ground.

"Open up that bag, Tex," Joe called, kneeling above his brother. "Let's see what's in it."

Tex didn't need to be told twice. He worked at the knotted drawstring that held the chamois bag closed, and when he got it loose, he tipped some of the contents out on his palm.

On the ground Al tried to wriggle free, but Joe tightened his grip and the other boy gasped and lay still. I saw his eyes as he looked up at us—as though he was hating us all.

Tex extended his palm and Florida and Galvin and I came close to stare at the glittering little objects that had tumbled from the bag. They were jewels. Jewels set into rings—diamonds, emeralds, rubies, sapphires. But mainly diamonds—quite large diamonds that shone even in the gray mist.

Joe let Al go and stood up. His brother rolled over and got stiffly to his feet, brushing himself off. He was beaten now and he knew it, but he had to take a stand and be cocky in spite of everything.

"Too bad," he said. "You sure spoiled things for us, Joe. There's enough there to send you through college and maybe keep us for a long time, even if you never picked up another guitar. We couldn't keep all that money, but these would have been worth more—and nobody knew they were there. Well, I guess that's that. I guess we'd better get on with that rehearsal or Jim will be sore. We need him now."

The way he could change face was astonishing. Here he was—hardly looking as though he had been in a fight, and acting as though everything was just as it had been before. He started for the tunnel, jaunty and mocking, but I knew that everything was different now and that he could not go on being Al Buddy.

Joe watched him climb toward the tunnel and he looked both angry and a little sad. When his brother was out of sight, he spoke to Galvin. "I always wondered if there really was a bag of rings. There's been a story handed around in our family about it. Along with a diagram of where the stuff was supposed to be hidden. My father always believed that Burt Boyd managed a big jewel robbery in New York before he took off for New Hampshire. Al has had it in his head for a long time that he wanted to track the story down. This invitation from Camberhills played right into his hands, and he sure has had me worried."

"What about you?" I couldn't help asking that. "How did you feel about those rings?"

Joe managed what was almost a smile. "I guess that's not the way I want to go to college," he said.

After that things happened pretty fast. Somebody showed Joe how to get out of the tunnel and he went after his brother. Galvin returned to the place where Old Beak Nose had once stood and got the packet of money. He said the rings must be turned over to the police, but there was no doubt about where that packet of bank money must go — right away!

We all headed for the gray house on the cliff and nobody argued about who should deliver the find. Even Chipper came along. We had all had a part in what happened. If Tex hadn't found the rock that looked like a nose, if Florida hadn't distracted Al Buddy, the ending might not have been so happy. Come to think of it, old Mr. Petrarch should have been there too. But when Galvin told his great-grandfather what had happened, he made it sound as if most of the credit was due me.

Mr. Putney held both my hands tightly and wasn't ashamed of the tears that rolled down his face. Rosalie Sewell kissed me warmly and put her cheek against mine. I knew she was crying too. Or I was. I couldn't tell which.

That moment was the very best part of the whole adventure. It was the real reward for all of us. But there was still more to come. Back home with the Myricks the whole story had to be told again, and after that the man from the paper came up to interview me — and this time I didn't mind. Then there were all sorts of phone calls, into and out of the house, including one to my mother and father. Mr. Myrick forgot about Athens because he said a better story was going on right here and he didn't want to miss any of it. The only time he got a little mad was when it came out that Florida and Tex had wanted that money for him.

We were all sitting in the kitchen once more, around plates of chocolate-chip ice cream, and Mr. Myrick got up from his chair and gave a small lecture.

"This is to give notice to my family," he said, " — once and for all! I am going to write what I feel like writing — whether it's a mystery or a love story or a Western or whatever. No one else can tell me what I ought to be writing. No writer worth his salt starts out to write an Important Book. He has something to say that comes out of him. He has a story to tell, and he does the very best he can with the material in hand. So I don't want to hear any more about how I'm wasting my time and ought to write something somebody else thinks is better. And that goes for your editor father, too, Trina. I'm an entertainer—a storyteller. And that's a profession I like. So let's not have any more talk about how we must get some money ahead in order to give poor old Pop a chance. O.K., everybody? Is that clear?"

Mrs. Myrick said, "Of course, dear," and Tex glared at his sister, who had, as usual, led him astray. Only Florida didn't seem to mind.

"Dad, I love your books!" she protested, and we all laughed together. No more was said about Mr. Myrick writing anything but what he wanted to write.

The affair was not yet over for me. I found that out on the opening night of the Folk Festival. A good crowd filled the meetinghouse and Al and Joe turned into being the Buddy Brothers again. The one thing that all of us had suppressed, when we talked to reporters who came in to write up the dramatic ending to the Big Bank Robbery, was how Al Buddy had behaved. About that we said nothing. He had taken a wrong course and he was getting his own special punishment. Joe was so disgusted with him that he had decided to break up the team right after the festival. Al would have to manage on his own, while Joe went back to school in September. If Al had saved so little of all that money he had made, it was his fault and he would have to figure out a way to earn his living—since no one would want one Buddy Brother. That was what Joe told him. Al just smiled and shrugged. I thought of his jangle about knowing so much, and thought he might just possibly be wrong. Maybe Al was the sort of boy who learned something only when it was too late.

At that moment, however, the Buddy Brothers were still the star performers of the festival. The program opened up with the local kids' group, and then a girl folk singer from Louisiana came on. After that, Mr. Davidson got up on the platform and thanked everyone for coming and told about the interesting plans he had for Goblin Glen. While he was talking I looked down the front row toward Galvin to see how he was taking this, but he winked at me, and I knew he didn't care anymore.

Mr. Davidson launched into a big thing about the Boyds and the Horsts meeting once more in Camberhills — with the past wiped out and made up for by Will's and Burt's descendants. Before I knew what he intended, he leaned right down from the platform to thank me in person — where I was sitting in the front row with the Myricks and Galvin and his sister. It was almost like my dream coming true. Except that the big moment was still to come — something I'd never dreamed of in my wildest fantasy.

When he had thanked me, Mr. Davidson introduced — not the Buddy Brothers — but just Joe Boyd. And Joe came up on the platform with his old wooden guitar that could make real music without any microphone or electrical hookup. He came to the front of the platform and looked down at me, smiling more warmly than I had ever thought he could.

"This is a jangle," he said. "And Miss Trina Corey will know what I mean, since I made it up for her."

He strummed a few accompanying bars and began to sing and I listened to him with my face growing as red as my hair, and prickles running up and down my spine.

> "Some girls big, some girls small,
>   Some girls tiny, some girls tall —
>   The one I like the best of all
>   Is Trina of Camberhills.

> "Trina has a plot, Trina has a plan,
>   She will find treasure if anyone can!
>   She's had a dream since it all began
>   With a treasure hunt in Camberhills."

There was quite a bit more, but I was too excited to hear half of it. Imagine having Joe Buddy write a song for me — and then set it to music! How could I hear anything? I was too busy feeling. Luckily he wrote it all down for me afterward, and even signed it for me with his real name.

When he was done and everyone was through applauding, the program went on. By that time I had a suspicion that the rest of the summer was going to be awfully dull by comparison. What could we do after solving a bank robbery and meeting the Buddy Brothers in person? I didn't even have Galvin as a project anymore.

I glanced down the row at him again and saw that he was thumping out the rhythm of electric guitars with his fingers on one knee. And I saw something else that made me look at him as hard as I could and blink my eyes. It wasn't possible — it couldn't be! But there was the evidence — just the beginning of evidence. Galvin had combed his hair in a slightly different way. He was letting it grow!

I almost choked with laughter as I turned to Florida sitting next to me, meaning to nudge her. The look on her face stopped me. Her mouth was set in a straight line, and she was staring off at nothing. I had a feeling that she was getting things all wrong again. She was probably figuring that nice things happened to me because I was thin, and brooding because she was fat.

Right then a new idea came along to occupy me. Words began to play themselves over and over in my mind. The words Joe Buddy had set to music: "Trina has a plot, Trina has a plan . . ."

Both Buddy Brothers were up on the platform now and under cover of their singing, I leaned over and nudged Florida.

"That was wonderful — what you did the other day. The way you saved everything by distracting Al down in the glen," I whispered. "If you hadn't done that, I don't know what might have happened."

She threw me a look that put me right in my place. Then she leaned over and whispered back.

"I've just found out I don't like this kind of music much," she said. "I guess it bores me."

I slid down a little in my seat and stopped trying to be president. Florida could look out for herself and perhaps it would be better if the affair of Goblin Glen didn't go to my head. It might even be a good idea if I relaxed for a while and just enjoyed the summer. But I certainly felt mixed up. Galvin was growing his hair, and Florida was bored by the Buddy Brothers!

On the platform Al and Joe were singing "How Do I Get Along?" and I watched them curiously. This was their last time on a stage together and I wasn't even crying. Did that mean that I was changing too?

Perhaps this was what growing up meant. Perhaps it simply meant letting old things go when you wore them out, and trying on new ideas, new interests — until you found the ones that really fit. And it didn't hurt very much, after all. I still loved what Joe Buddy had done for me, but now I began to look forward to the summer and getting to know Florida and Tex and Galvin a whole lot better. Maybe I might even get to know me a little better.

About Phyllis A. Whitney

SOMETIMES people ask Phyllis A. Whitney about the "A" in her name. Her mother thought it would be nice to give her a Japanese flower name since she was born in Japan, so her middle name is Ayame (pronounced Ah-yah-meh). It is the word for iris in Japanese.

Phyllis Whitney was born in Yokohama, of American parents. She lived in Japan, China, and the Philippine Islands until she was fifteen. After her father's death her mother brought her home to the United States for the first time. Here they lived for two years in Berkeley, California, and then moved to San Antonio, Texas. Phyllis was seventeen when her mother died and she went to Chicago to live with an aunt.

For many years her home was in Staten Island, in the harbor of New York City, and several of her books have had a Staten Island background. In 1967, however, she and her husband bought a house near Sussex, New Jersey, in the northern corner of that state. After living in cities all her life, she finds that she likes the country better and enjoys walking in the woods and climbing the hills that are part of her present setting.

All her life she has wanted to be a writer, and her earliest stories were written when she was a child living in the Orient. Her first appearance in print was on the children's page of the famous *St. Nicholas Magazine*. When she grew up and had to earn a living—which usually cannot be done immediately by writing stories—she worked at a number of jobs connected with books: in a public library and in bookstores in Chicago.

Later she reviewed children's books for Chicago and Phila-delphia newspapers. She was a teacher of juvenile writing at Northwestern University and at New York University, where she helped many young writers toward publication.

Now that she can give all her time to writing, she alternates between books for young people and suspense novels for adults, several of which have been best sellers. Of her mysteries for girls and boys *Secret of the Tiger's Eye* won an Edgar (named for Edgar Allan Poe) from Mystery Writers of America. *Mystery of the Haunted Pool* won both an Edgar and the Sequoyah Award of Oklahoma.

She has one daughter, Georgia, and three grandchildren, Barbara, Michael, and Lorraine.

FRONT ENDPAPER
MISSING